ODD OCCURRENCES

ODD OCCURRENCES

CHILLING STORIES OF HORROR

ANDREW NANCE

WITH ILLUSTRATIONS BY JANA HEIDERSDORF

Christy Ottaviano Books

LITTLE, BROWN AND COMPANY
New York   Boston

Christy Ottaviano Books
Hachette Book Group
1290 Avenue of the Americas, New York, NY 10104
Visit us at LBYR.com

First Edition: September 2022

Christy Ottaviano Books is an imprint of Little, Brown and Company. The Christy Ottaviano Books name and logo are trademarks of Hachette Book Group, Inc.

Library of Congress Cataloging-in-Publication Data
Names: Nance, Andrew, author. | Heidersdorf, Jana, illustrator.
Title: Odd occurrences : chilling stories of horror / Andrew Nance, with illustrations by Jana Heidersdorf.
Description: First edition. | New York : Little, Brown and Company, 2022. | Audience: Ages 8-12 | Summary: A middle-grade collection of scary stories that weave into a larger mystery.
Identifiers: LCCN 2021062518 | ISBN 9780316334334 (hardcover) | ISBN 9780316334532 (ebook)
Subjects: CYAC: Horror stories. | Short stories. | LCGFT: Horror fiction. | Short stories.
Classification: LCC PZ7.N143 Od 2022 | DDC [Fic]—dc23
LC record available at https://lccn.loc.gov/2021062518

ISBNs: 978-0-316-33433-4 (hardcover), 978-0-316-33453-2 (ebook)

Printed in the United States of America

LSC-C

Printing 1, 2022

This book is dedicated to my lifelong friend, Wade. As kids we endlessly watched monster movies and told each other scary stories, much like the ones you'll find in this book.

Beware the Autumn people.

—Ray Bradbury, *Something Wicked This Way Comes*

CONTENTS

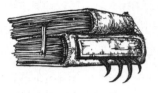

- CHAPTER 1 -

A PODCAST

"Happy, Halloween, Mrs. Ayers. Jana called and said she got some new stuff for the podcast."

"Come on in, Zeus." Jana's mom stepped aside to let me enter.

Zeus isn't my real name. Those paintings of the god Zeus show a big man with Conan-sized muscles, long white hair, and a beard slinging lightning bolts. I'm skinny and tall with dark, close-cropped hair. And if I tried to grab a lightning bolt, you could sweep up my remains with a broom and dustpan. My first name is Jesús, with the Hispanic pronunciation, *Hey-Zeus*. That's why everybody calls me Zeus.

Mrs. Ayers wore green pajamas with a light robe hanging

loose. "I don't know why you have to do your little show so late."

I gave Mrs. Ayers what I hoped was a charming smile despite her calling my podcast *your little show*. "Oh, nine o'clock isn't that late, and it's only once a week. I originally wanted to livestream it at midnight."

"And if it was that late, Jana couldn't be your assistant."

I held up my index finger. "She's not my assistant; she's the podcast's producer and engineer. That's a big difference."

"If you say so." Mrs. Ayers beckoned me inside and called up the stairs. "Jana, Zeus is here." She turned back to me. "So, is your listenership growing?"

"Yes, ma'am, a little more each week. Lots of kids want to share their stories."

"Oh, come on, Zeus, you don't really believe them, do you? I mean, really, ghosts and flying saucers and boogeymen."

For an answer, I just gave her a smile and a shrug. I did a podcast called *Odd Occurrences*, which we streamed live Saturday nights at nine o'clock. The recordings of those were available 24/7 as podcasts. I told the truth when I said our listenership was growing, but we still weren't a blip on the radar when compared with *TED Talks*, *The Moth*,

Casefile True Crime, Weird Darkness, and other podcasts. I guess one reason we were so little known was that you had to journey pretty far down the rabbit hole to find *Odd Occurrences.* First, you had to click on *Creepy Collections,* a website that offered links to supernatural websites, publications, photos, videos, and my podcast.

"Maybe you'd have more listeners if you didn't have such gruesome topics." She made a scrunched-up face as if there were a bad smell in the room.

I fought to keep from rolling my eyes. I'd had this debate with Jana's mom since we first started the podcast a year ago. What she called gruesome, I called fascinating. The paranormal. I'd always been into the supernatural, but even more so since a life-changing experience that I planned to talk about on our special Halloween podcast later tonight. And tied into my experience, I was searching for something, which was the main reason I started the show. There were a lot of podcasts about adults dealing with the paranormal, but *Odd Occurrences* was dedicated to kids who had supernatural events occur in their lives.

"I better go see what's holding up Jana," I said, and went upstairs.

Jana was in the hallway, two boxes in her hands, looking into the empty room in her house. A year older than me, she was tall and thin. This evening she wore her favorite ensemble: bib overalls, a T-shirt, and sneakers. Her brother, and my best friend, Tobin, used to tease her for wearing overalls everywhere.

"He used to call you Farm Girl when you wore overalls," I said, moving next to her, taking in the unused space.

"He sounds like a jerk," she said.

"And you called him that more than once."

Curiosity was plain on her face as she tucked a strand of her long burgundy hair behind an ear. "Did we fight a lot?"

"Nah. You never fought. Argued is a different story. But mostly you guys were really tight."

"Hmmm." She took in that bit of information, trying to get a grasp on who Tobin was, and their relationship. "You know, I always wanted a brother or sister."

"You had one. A brother."

She shrugged. "All I can remember is being an only child." She stared a little longer and then broke her reverie. "Oh hey, our new headphones came today." She handed me a box.

I looked at it. "Sennheisers, awesome."

Tobin and I had been best friends since kindergarten, which means I've known Jana a long time. She used to hang out with us a lot. It was pure luck that she had been visiting their grandparents when Carnival Nocturne came to town, otherwise she might be missing, too. Missing and forgotten. I've always liked her, but we've become a whole lot closer this past year. She'd gone from best friend's sister to good friend, and once I convinced her that what had happened to Tobin and me was true, we started working on how to get him back.

We went downstairs. "Remember, it's our special Halloween show tonight, Mom," Jana said. "It's going to be a late one; don't wait up."

"I remember," Mrs. Ayers said. "Promise me you won't go anywhere besides Zeus's."

Jana promised and we left. It was only a block's walk to my house, and we took our time checking out the neighbors' Halloween decorations. I stopped in front of the Sanderses' house. They always went all out for Halloween, Christmas, and the Fourth of July. They had a full-sized witch in black dress near the door. I knew from past years that it was motion-activated and would cackle and jerk around. Mr. Sanders had carved a dozen monster-face pumpkins and set them around the yard. There was a bunch of other cool things, but the creepiest by far was the doll he'd placed by the door.

The doll was obviously an antique that had seen better days. The tangled brunette hair looked real, and I remembered reading somewhere that they'd implant human hair in some of those old dolls. My guess was the dress used to be bright blue, but it was now faded and as dirty as if someone had buried it for the past year and dug it up for tonight. Its right foot was bare, and there was a small leather shoe on the left that was so torn and grimy that I wasn't sure what color it originally was. The spookiest part was the porcelain face. It had become dirt-stained over the decades, giving it a blotchy complexion. A spiderweb of cracks started from the center of the left cheek and spread out. The widest fissure ran up to a black hole where the left eye was supposed to be. The right eye was a vivid blue and reflected scrutiny, intelligence, and malevolence.

Jana had walked on and stopped. "What are you looking at?"

"That doll," I said. "I think I saw it last Halloween, but I don't remember it being here."

She studied it a moment. "At least it's not a clown. I hate clowns. Let's go; we've got to prep."

Once at my house, we went inside for supplies. While Jana talked with my parents, I went into the kitchen, put a cooler on the kitchen table, and loaded it with snacks, bottled water, soda, and a couple of energy drinks to help us stay awake.

My older brother strolled into the kitchen with his backpack over a shoulder. "Your big show tonight, huh?"

"Yep."

He dropped his backpack next to the cooler and knocked over the saltshaker.

"Geez, Eric. Tonight of all nights?"

My brother laughed. "You and your superstitions. Just why is spilling salt supposed to be bad luck?"

"It goes back thousands of years," I said.

"Sure it does," he said sarcastically.

"Legend has it that right before he betrayed Jesus, Judas Iscariot spilled salt at the last supper. Da Vinci even included it in his famous painting of Christ's last meal." I took a pinch of the spilled salt and tossed it over my left shoulder.

"And why's that supposed to counter the bad luck?"

"Supposedly the devil lurks behind your left shoulder. Throw a little salt in his eyes and you blind him."

Eric laughed. "You oughta write the Encyclopedia of Superstitions. Well, here's mine: *Break a leg* tonight." He didn't really want me to snap a bone; he was big into plays and musicals at the high school, and "break a leg" was an actor's way of saying good luck.

"Thanks, bro." I wasn't just superstitious, I was a superstition know-it-all. No one is 100 percent sure where "break a leg" originated, and there are several theories. The most likely explanation is that a lot of actors are very superstitious. They believed if you wished a fellow actor good luck, it would actually bring bad luck. So saying something bad, like "break a leg," would be good luck. I know it doesn't make any sense, but with actors, you're dealing with people who will not say the name of Shakespeare's *Macbeth* out loud in a theater because it supposedly guarantees their show will be a flop.

I got Jana, and we went out the back door to the shed that my father had let me turn into a studio. Once I escaped from the mirrors, a year ago on this very night, I spent the next several weeks coming up with a plan to find Carnival Nocturne. That's why I started the podcast. Jana helped me set it up. Lucky for me, she's a tech nerd.

Jana had said the first thing our studio needed was sound dampeners. "If we don't use them, our podcast will have a tinny, hollow sound."

We went online and learned that acoustic tiles are really expensive. Jana had a brainstorm, and we bought cheap rolls of upholstery foam and covered the walls with that. We got a used soundboard from a local DJ. Then we picked up the kind of microphones used by online gamers.

I sat in my big, comfortable, rolling office chair that I'd gotten when one of my neighbors put it out with the trash. A half dozen strips of silver duct tape covered all the tears in the leather. Opening the box, I pulled out my new headphones. Checking them over, I plugged them into the jack box that we'd attached under our big square table. I adjusted the microphone that hung at the end of a flexible boom clamped to the table edge. Though I was well aware of the upcoming segments we would broadcast, Jana handed me a clipboard with a list of people we'd prerecorded via the phone. These were kids from all over the world, talking about the weird, supernatural, and frightening things that had happened to them.

Jana took her place across the table and switched on the soundboard, worked her magic with the laptop we used for streaming, adjusted her mic, checked sound levels, and did other prep work.

I took a moment to look at the framed picture that hung on the opposite wall. I'd drawn it. Being an artist, I never knew when something would inspire me to draw, so I always carried my sketch pad and charcoal pencils in my backpack. The one on the wall was a drawing of Tobin in mid-leap on his skateboard. I had to sketch it from memory because when I returned from Carnival Nocturne, no one remembered him, not even his family. All evidence of a kid named Tobin had vanished. One of the weirdest things was that he was no longer in any photographs. Those photos still existed, but his image was erased.

Next to the picture of Tobin was a framed eleven-by-fourteen-inch mirror. I knew the exact dimensions because that was also the size of the paper in my sketch pads. Hidden on the flip side, and attached with Velcro, was a map that would help me save Tobin—if I got the chance.

When I had escaped and returned, the hardest thing for me to accept was that even Jana didn't remember Tobin.

"Who?" she'd asked.

By that point, we'd gone round and round as I tried explaining to her what had happened. Frustration had set in, and I yelled, "Your brother!"

"I don't have a brother!" she shouted back.

"Gah!" I roared and left.

She called after me, "If you really believe that stuff, you should see a doctor!"

Over the next few days, I obsessed about how to get

Jana to believe me. I went over one day while her parents were at work and rang the doorbell. She had opened the door, saw it was me, and started to close it again.

"Wait." I held up my hands. "I'm sorry I lost my temper the other day. I know I came at you hard, but I was upset. I'd just gotten out of the mirrors."

"I don't know what you're talking about, Zeus. Unless this is some stupid prank. If it is, it's not going to work."

"Give me just a few minutes," I said. "If you still don't believe me, I won't bother you ever again."

"Go ahead," she said reluctantly.

"Remember that concert we went to a couple of months ago?" I asked.

"Sure, the Palmetto Music Festival."

"Doesn't it strike you as odd that we went together?"

"We've done lots of stuff together."

"Yeah, but why do you hang out with a boy a year younger than you? Wouldn't it make more sense if your younger brother and I were good friends and that's why?"

I was happy to see she was actually thinking about it, but she didn't answer.

I pushed past her and ran up the staircase. She followed. I stopped at Tobin's bedroom door and opened it. I held out both hands to the room as if making a point.

"It's a room, so what?" Jana had said.

"Don't you think it's strange there's nothing in here? No furniture, no pictures, no...anything? You've lived here for thirteen years, as long as you've been alive. In all that time, your parents have never done anything with this room. No guest bedroom, no office, not even a storage room."

Again, I could tell she was running that through her head. "I guess that is a little strange."

"It's because this is your brother's room. Because he's stuck in the mirrors, he no longer exists in our world."

"I don't know." She was starting to doubt again.

I grabbed her wrist and pulled her after me, downstairs and to the living room, where her mother displayed a couple dozen family photos. "Look at all those pictures."

"I don't have to. I see them every day."

"Humor me." When she stared at one, I said, "Notice that space between you and your mother."

She sighed. "So?"

"That space is big enough that someone could have been standing there and then was somehow, I don't know, erased from it."

"Oh come on, Zeus. You're not making sense."

"Look at them all. Every one of them has an empty space big enough for Tobin."

Jana went from picture to picture, her face growing paler.

I took off my backpack and got my sketchbook from it, showing her the rendering I'd made of Tobin on his skateboard.

I spoke like I was pleading, desperate for her to believe me. "This is Tobin; this is your brother. I drew it from memory so I wouldn't forget what he looked like."

She took the sketchbook and stared at the picture for minutes, finally muttering, "There is a family resemblance."

"I know it's bizarre, I know it's not possible, and I know it's true. All I ask is that you think about it. Consider the possibility."

Three days later, my doorbell rang. I opened the door, and Jana stood on the welcome mat. She looked confused and a little scared as she said the best thing possible: "I believe you."

She was the only one. And she's been helping me ever since in my plan to find the carnival and get Tobin back. Sometimes I'll catch her standing in front of my drawing, trying to remember him.

I shook off the memory when Jana announced, "Thirty seconds."

I put on my headphones and spoke into the mic so that Jana could set my levels. "Test, check. One, two, three. Test, test, check. Wow, these headphones sound great."

She gave me a thumbs-up and turned her attention to the analog clock on the wall. Second by second, the time ticked down to nine o'clock. Finally, she held up her hand showing me five fingers, then four, then three, then two, and then she pointed at me.

As with each show, I had a little superstitious ritual, and before I did anything else, I knocked on the wooden table for good luck. I let several seconds of our theme song, "Funeral March of a Marionette," play before speaking into my microphone. "Happy Halloween and welcome to *Odd Occurrences*, streaming live each Saturday night at nine, Eastern Standard Time, or you can listen to any of our podcasts whenever you want through our host website, *Creepy Collections*. If you've listened before, you know we open and close each podcast by passing along the number for the Carnival Nocturne hotline. If Carnival Nocturne is set up in your town or city, I ask you to please call. The number is 386-555-3822.

"Normally, each *Odd Occurrences* podcast lasts an hour. Tonight, we have something special planned. And by *we*, I'm referring to myself and my producer-slash-engineer,

Jana." We do the same stupid joke each week. "Say hello, Jana."

She said, "Hello, Jana." Like I said, a stupid joke. Then she continued, "We have a very special night planned in honor of Halloween. Instead of getting out in the neighborhood and trick-or-treating, Zeus and I will be here in the *Odd Occurrences* studio until we've broadcast all the cool stories we've collected for the night. Stories that really happened to kids from all around the world, odd occurrences that could very well, someday, happen to you." She followed that with a stinger, an orchestra playing a suspenseful *bum-bum-bummmmmm*. "We have nine stories from podcast listeners tonight and another one from our host, Zeus. It's a terrifying adventure that inspired him to start this podcast. So, ten scary stories in total for Halloween. In our production meeting, I suggested that we make it thirteen odd occurrences. Thirteen is a much more potent number when discussing the paranormal, and certainly creepier."

"And I said no, because thirteen is also an unlucky number."

"It's just a superstition, Zeus."

"And I'm superstitious, so I nixed thirteen, and we're keeping it to the ten stories you'll hear tonight."

"You're the boss," Jana said. "As you know, Zeus and I seek out kids who claim that odd events happened to them. What you don't know is that we've saved the best and most disturbing for tonight's *Odd Occurrences*. They've been prerecorded, and we'll play them for you as this special Halloween night unfolds. It will be a late night for Zeus, me, and you, our listeners."

Jana started a music bed, music played softly enough so someone could talk over it. We regularly scoured the internet for royalty-free music, and we'd found several sites that kept us supplied with weird tunes. A good music bed can add a bit of showmanship, emotion, and intensity to what's said. The bed she played was a calliope, the antique steam organ that's played at carnivals and circuses. Usually a happy sound, this one played a sinister tune, echoing in a creepy fashion and uncertain tempo, and the notes were slightly out of tune. It was also the ringtone we'd selected for the Carnival Nocturne hotline. We'd planned tonight's show for weeks, but at this moment, I was sweating and having a hard time catching my breath. I was doubting I could share my story with so many people. My mouth opened and closed, but nothing came out.

Jana watched me for long seconds, and finally opened her mic. In a soft voice, she said, "Zeus, you've put it off long enough. Time to tell our listeners about Carnival Nocturne and why you have a hotline dedicated to finding it."

Had she not been there, offering up moral support, I think I would have bailed on my story and just played the prerecorded ones. But finally, I said, "Something happened to me a year..." My voice was raspy, as my mouth had gone dry. I twisted the top off a bottle of water and drank. Taking a deep breath, I focused on starting the story. "The reason I have the Carnival Nocturne hotline is because of what happened exactly one year ago, on Halloween, to me and to my good friend Tobin, Jana's brother. A person nobody remembers except for me."

Jana cast her eyes down.

"I'm not picking on you, Jana." I explained to our listeners, "She feels guilty that she can't remember Tobin, but she believes me."

"I do," Jana shot back.

"The reason I'm the only one who remembers Tobin, I think, is because I was there with him when we went to Carnival Nocturne and into the House of Mystery and Mirrors. If you're going to be stuck inside a nightmare, Tobin's definitely who you'd want with you. He's like coiled energy compressed into a body, energy that could, at any moment, explode into manic action. Yeah, his grades were always in the tank, but he's smart and shrewd, which was a benefit in the mirrors. And just so you can picture him in your mind, he's shorter than me, and I'm five feet five inches. Tobin is solid and strong. His hair is long and light brown, with streaks of blond, and because he's a surfer, it's styled by salt water. When we went into the mirrors, Tobin wore orange swim trunks, having gotten in some surfing earlier in the day. His green tank top was from a music festival we had attended a couple of months earlier with Jana.

"Now that you have that image of Tobin in your mind, I'll tell you what happened to us throughout the podcast tonight. It'll be hard for me to put into words, but I swear it's all true." I looked at Jana, cleared my throat, and took another big swig, emptying the water bottle.

"Okay, here's what happened."

CHAPTER 2

THE HOUSE OF MYSTERY AND MIRRORS (PART 1)

The carnival came to town without warning. There were no COMING SOON posters, no online announcements, and nothing in the newspaper. Like a community leveled by a tornado, we learned of it only by its arrival. It just appeared.

Tobin texted me, Hit the waves with Kevin this morning. He says there's a carnival in town.

Ten minutes later, we were headed for the city's special-events field. My bike's a rusted black beach cruiser with big tires for getting through the sand. Tobin had a hold of my seat and was pulled along on his skateboard.

"Too bad Jana's at your grandparents," I said.

"Yeah, she's gonna miss all the fun."

As we made our way up the incline of the bridge over the waterway, Tobin helped our momentum by pushing with his foot while I stood and pedaled. Once we reached the top, it was a fast trip coasting down the other side. We had a nice, wide bike lane, but a tourist in a straw hat, flowery shirt, pleated shorts, flip-flops, and black socks was strolling along, blocking that lane. I glanced behind at the traffic and timed it so we arrived at the two-legged roadblock between cars. I whipped the bike around him without slowing.

Tobin pointed at the concrete to our right. "Hey, buddy, why do you think they call that a sidewalk?"

I glanced back as the startled man stumbled onto the curb. Good ol' Tobin, doing his part for traffic safety in our seaside community of Crescent Harbor.

The special-events field was at the outskirts of town on the other side of downtown. A five-acre plot where the city held festivals, concerts, farmers markets, and art gatherings. I took a roundabout route and ended up slowing down as we went by Katie Courtney's house. I was hoping she'd be out and we could stop and talk to her. I didn't see her in her yard and picked up speed as Tobin gave me grief about having a crush on her. Still, it was worth riding through the neighborhood, because everyone had their Halloween decorations out. I stopped for a moment at one house. It was a simple brick ranch, nice yard, a couple of trees, and only one decoration. Sitting up on a limb was an antique doll with a cracked face and dirty dress.

"What?" Tobin asked.

I pointed at the doll. "That should win an award for best Halloween decoration."

"Creepy. But one doll shouldn't win out over the Sanderses' Halloween extravaganza."

I studied it as I'd study anything I was about to sketch. "I don't know. The juxtaposition of that one repulsive doll with such an ordinary house really stands out."

"The juxtapo-whazzit?" Tobin asked.

"It's the effect of two things together that project a stark contrast so that—"

"Okay, genius, keep pedaling; we've got a carnival to get to."

I laughed and started off. Because of our reroute, we approached the special-events field from the west, and both the west and north sides of the field were surrounded by woods.

As we passed a portion of the woods, I got my first glimpse. "The field's empty. There's no carnival."

"Kevin said it was here." Tobin stood on tiptoes on his skateboard. "Wait a minute. Look."

Once we cleared the trees at the west end, we saw that the carnival was indeed there, but not on the field. In the corner where the north woods met the west woods was a big black sign with fancy gold script: CARNIVAL NOCTURNE. Under the sign was an entrance into the woods. On each side of the entrance were big canvas paintings advertising what awaited inside.

"Where is everybody?" I asked.

When we hit the dirt, Tobin hopped off his skateboard. With a kick of his foot, the skateboard flipped into the air, and he caught it. "I don't think anyone knows about it yet. Kevin only knew because his mom drove by this morning while taking him to the beach."

I parked my bike near the entrance, and Tobin put his skateboard under it.

We could hear the clanging of what we took to be tent spikes being hammered into the ground. The aroma of someone cooking with pungent spices filled the air. We spent time looking at the canvas signs. The same fancy script spelled out THE EXCEPTIONALS on one. Underneath the lettering was a painting of a group of individuals with unique features.

"Hang on." I took off my backpack, which had a lucky rabbit's foot hanging from a loop, and pulled out my sketch pad and a charcoal pencil. Tobin sighed with impatience. I ignored him and started sketching some of the strange people on the sign, including a woman who, instead of a human nose and mouth, had a bird's beak like an eagle. I drew twin girls with scaled skin who were pictured with their arms around each other. Another I sketched was a man with two heads. I also did a rendering of a teenager with a human face and a body like a frog.

Tobin watched me and said, "I dub thee Frog Boy." He had a habit of assigning people nicknames based on appearance. It had gotten us into trouble on more than one occasion.

The last one I sketched was a man lying like a jungle cat with his head up and looking straight out. Dark-skinned, he had the ears of a big cat, and his eyes were gold with vertical black pupils.

"I'll call him Man Panther...no wait...Manther." Tobin looked at me and said, "You are such a slob."

I looked down at my T-shirt and grinned self-consciously.

It was a running joke. When I sketched, I added shading by spreading the charcoal with my fingers. I'd then subconsciously wipe my fingers on my shirt. Mom gave me grief over it. One time, when Tobin was at the house and she was doing laundry, she held up one of my smudged T-shirts and said, *I don't know why you do that. You're not a slob.* So now Tobin calls me a slob when I do it.

"Slob and proud of it."

Tobin started bobbing up and down on his feet and sounded like an impatient little kid. "Come on, Zeus. Let's look around."

I could have stood there and done more sketches, as a lot more Exceptionals were depicted on the sign. But I put my drawing tools in my backpack and slung it over my shoulder. "Okay, let's go."

We started for the entrance, but I stopped at the final sign. Gilt letters spelled out SEE THE ONE AND ONLY HOUSE OF MYSTERY AND MIRRORS. There was a depiction of a dark, two-story house, though it wasn't clearly visible, like it was sitting in thick fog.

Tobin threw an arm over my shoulders and dragged me along to a thick burgundy rope hung across the entrance to the woods. A sign dangled from the rope: OPEN AT SUNSET.

"Ah bummer," Tobin said. We could see a number of large, colorful tents among the trees. "Maybe we can still go in. You know, look around and stuff." Before I could protest, Tobin passed under the rope and took a step forward. Immediately, the clanging stopped and a shadow approached from the woods. As it got closer, it turned into a very large, heavily muscled man.

Tobin then took two steps back. "Whoa."

The man was over seven feet tall, and he hefted a sledgehammer so big that I doubted I could have lifted it. He passed it from one hand to the other with an easy grip as he looked at us. He swung the sledgehammer up and settled it across his broad shoulders, his muscles on full display in his sweat-stained tank top. With a shaved head, he wore a gold hoop earring in each lobe. There were gold rings on each of his fingers and both thumbs. He stood with a wide stance in gray pants that were tucked into calf-high lace-up boots.

"Hi there, Big Guy." There he went with the nickname thing again. I glanced at the big man; he didn't seem to mind.

"Maybe you better get back on this side of the rope," I said.

Tobin stared at the man some more and then whispered

to me, "I'll ask Big Guy if we can take a look around." He took a step forward.

The large man smiled, revealing a gold front tooth. He released his grip on the sledgehammer with his right hand and waggled that index finger back and forth like a metronome. I noted that his finger was almost as thick as my wrist.

"Or maybe not," Tobin said, and stepped back under the rope.

The man took the sledgehammer from his shoulder and flung it high enough that it spun three times before he caught it one-handed. He put it over a shoulder and headed back to the woods.

"Hey! Great chatting with you. We'll be back tonight," Tobin called after the man.

We turned. Tobin gasped and I yelped. A woman stood just behind us. She was beautiful, with lush black hair reflecting the sunlight. Her eyes were large and so blue they bordered on violet.

"Hello, boys," she said. Her voice was deep and smoky, and her lips held an amused smile. "I didn't mean to scare you."

"Just didn't know you were there," Tobin croaked.

"Surprised us is all," I added.

She was barefoot and wore jeans and a peasant blouse the same color as her eyes. She held up her hand, turning it one way and another, showing that it was empty. She passed her other hand in front of it, her long, slender fingers dancing in motion, and, like magic, she held two tickets.

"Admission for two surprised young men. I am Queen of the Carnival, matriarch of the House of Mystery and Mirrors. I promise an experience you'll never forget."

I reached out and took the tickets from her. She walked between us and touched each of our noses as she passed. Ducking under the rope, she made her way into the woods.

We returned that night to Carnival Nocturne.

"Word got out," Tobin said.

"Yep." The parking lot was full, and people were streaming into the woods through the carnival entrance.

Colored lights radiated from deep in the woods, reds and blues, purples and yellows. The closer we got to the entrance, the louder the music. It wasn't regular carnival fare, but more hypnotic, with lots of stringed instruments and percussion.

We joined the flow of townsfolk and found ourselves at narrow ticket booths, two to each side. They were dark inside, and we couldn't see the ticket takers. We held out our tickets, and pale, skeletal hands emerged from the booth windows and snatched them from our fingers.

We entered, and Tobin turned in a circle, his eyes big. It was awesome to be immersed in that atmosphere of richly hued lights, colorful tents, mesmerizing music, and the aroma of exotic food, crowded with people, including carnival workers in their bright and shiny costumes. I'd been to a number of county fairs and small carnivals, and they all seemed dirty, tired, and worn. Everything at Carnival Nocturne was immaculate.

"This is so much cooler than trick-or-treating," I said.

"Definitely," Tobin agreed.

While Tobin absorbed it all with glee, I looked around wondering how, in such a short time, they had cleared out the woods. The trees remained, but all the brush and debris on the ground had been removed, leaving us to walk on hard-packed dirt. I shrugged, and we went farther into the carnival. Paper lanterns were strung overhead in the trees, marking out the paths. We got to a crossroads crowded with people. We were deciding which way to go when what felt like a twenty-pound slab of meat dropped onto my shoulder. I glanced down at a monstrous hand with gold rings. Another hand rested on Tobin. We turned around and looked up at the huge man we'd seen earlier that day. A gold tooth twinkled with his smile. He wore a red shirt made from enough silk to fashion a ship's sail. Tight black pants were tucked into black boots. Instead of a belt, an iridescent blue sash was tied around his waist.

"S'up, Big Guy?" Tobin said.

He released us and pointed to the trail leading to the left. "The rides." His voice was deep and growly. If a grizzly bear could speak, I imagined it would sound like him. Pointing straight ahead, he said, "The shows." His accent placed his origin somewhere in eastern Europe. He aimed his finger at the right trail. "The House of Mystery and Mirrors."

"Thanks?" I said, like a question.

Big Guy laughed, then slapped our backs so hard that we stumbled a couple of steps forward.

When he left, I got my sketch pad from my backpack and showed Tobin the drawing I'd made earlier of Big Guy, pictured with his sledgehammer on his shoulder.

"You nailed it," Tobin said.

"Yeah? Check this one out." I flipped to a page where I'd sketched the Queen of the Carnival.

He looked at it for a long moment. "You got some serious skills, Zeus. Don't forget your friends when you become a famous artist."

I punched his shoulder. "I'd never forget you. It's like Dad says, you're my brother from another mother."

After a brief discussion, we chose the left path, to the rides. We'd taken only a half dozen steps when I stopped and bent down to pick up a penny.

Tobin shook his head. "A penny isn't going to buy you anything."

"The value of a found penny doesn't have anything to do with money."

"Let me guess; it's good luck?"

"You got it, especially if it's a heads-up penny."

"Along with skills, you got some quirks," Tobin said.

"It gives me character," I said, and smiled.

We started with a series of zip lines. Next was a 300-step spiral staircase to a slide that ended up being every bit as fast and thrilling as a roller coaster. It wound its way through the trees, twisted through lefts and rights, corkscrewed down, and even sent us in a full loop-de-loop.

The Ferris wheel sat in a clearing and was powered by two strong men who turned cranks on either side of a large gear, which was connected by a big chain to an even bigger gear. And that was connected to a gear at the center, which spun the Ferris wheel around.

Vowing to return for more rides, we headed for the

shows. At the crossroads, we turned left onto a long path that led deep into the woods with big brightly colored tents on each side. We peeked into each one we passed.

"Is it just me?" Tobin said. "Or do the tents look bigger on the inside than out?"

"They do," I said.

We stopped before another tent with a sign saying it was the site of THE EXCEPTIONALS. A rope hung across the entrance, from which a sign dangled. NEXT SHOW AT TEN O'CLOCK.

"I want to see this one." I checked the time on my cell phone. "Forty minutes."

Something small hit my back. I turned to see a shadowy figure standing under a tree, which blocked the light of a nearby lantern. The person used his right hand to toss a small projectile that hit Tobin on the shoulder and got his attention. When they stepped from the shadow, I saw it was two people. Or was it one person? I remembered the sign with the group painting of The Exceptionals. One was a two-headed man, and here he—they—were, under a tree by the tent. The right-hand head nodded a greeting. The two faces were almost identical. They were handsome in a 1930s movie star kind of way, with sharp features and dark, slicked-back hair. The only difference was the right-side head sported a mustache. The right hand was

cupped, and it came up, tossing something into the right-side head's mouth.

The left-side head said, "Boiled peanuts? Ugh. Do you know how much salt they use? Do you know what you're doing to our blood pressure?"

The right head chewed and smiled. Turning to us, he gestured at the other head with the hand holding the peanuts. "He's such a Goody Two-shoes." His voice was smooth but nasal. He—they—wore a black tuxedo. Pushing from the tree, left hand in his trouser pocket, the head with the mustache said, "How ya kids doing? We ain't wearing no Halloween costume; what you see is what you get. My name is Winston; the gentleman beside me is Hume."

"Pleased to meet you," the other head, Hume, said.

"Y-e-e-e-a-a-a-h-h-h-h," Tobin drew out the word.

"Uh-huh," was all I managed.

Winston tossed more peanuts into his mouth and said, "You ever see those cartoons where someone has a big decision to make?" He chewed. "An angel appears on one shoulder, encouraging 'em to make the right decision, and then a little devil pops up in a puff of smoke on the other shoulder telling him to make the wrong decision, which, by the way, is usually the fun one. Well, to give you a hint, I'd be the one carrying the pitchfork." He winked at us and pointed toward the tent. "For most of the nineteenth and twentieth century, circuses and carnivals would call that a freak show and call Hume and me a freak. Insulting, huh? Here at Carnival Nocturne, our uniqueness is celebrated. Hence, we're called The Exceptionals. We hope you'll see our show. Right, Hume?"

"Too true, too true," Hume said. "However, I think we both agree that before you come back for our show, you should visit the Oracle."

A man and woman holding hands walked past. "Look!" the woman said, staring at Winston and Hume. "That is so gross."

The man leaned in and whispered to the woman, and they both snickered as they continued down the walkway.

"We get that a lot," Hume said.

"Jerks," Tobin muttered. He then asked, "The Oracle? Where's that?"

Winston stepped forward and threw his peanuts hard into the back of the man's head.... "That direction."

The couple stopped, and the man turned angry eyes our way. "Hey!"

The two-headed man stepped forward. Hume chewed a left-hand fingernail as Winston looked at the man through narrowed eyes, his lips twisted into a sneer. "What?"

The man's indignity deflated, and he turned and ush-
ered his date on.

"Yeah, that's right. Welcome to Carnival Nocturne,"
he called after them. The two-headed man walked past
us, and before he—they—disappeared into the tent, he—
they—gave us a little salute. Winston said, "See you two
sooner than you'd like."

Tobin's confused look turned into a broad smile. "This
place is incredible. Let's go see the Oracle."

It was slow going through the carnival crowd, but we
finally reached the last of the paper lanterns.

"Did you see any signs about the Oracle at any of the
tents?" I asked.

"Nope," Tobin said.

The path continued on, but in darkness. I was about to
suggest we head back up and double-check every tent
when a shaft of light appeared farther down the dark
path. Someone had opened a tent flap, allowing light to
escape. Two kids our age emerged. One was small, the
other a bit taller but much wider.

"Oh no," I said, and stopped.

"Yep. Looks like Vince and Nash."

A couple of trouble-makers from school. If bullying
were a school subject, they'd have 4.0s. They'd also have

perfect grades in Shoplifting 101 and Advanced Vandalism. Vince was the bigger of the two.

Laughing, they headed toward us. Vince carried something in his hands.

A third figure stumbled from the tent. The man was stooped and wore a robe with a hood pulled up. A weak voice called out, "Wait, you can't take those. You'll get me in trouble."

Vince turned back. "Then you shoulda given me a good fortune."

"I don't create the fortunes; it's in the cards," the old man said.

Vince held up the cards. "Then I'll take them and make my own." He laughed, and Nash echoed him.

"Come on," Tobin said with a grim expression.

I followed him, and in a few seconds, we stood before Vince and Nash.

Vince sneered. "Don't go in there; it's a rip-off."

As the old man shuffled up, Tobin said, "Give him his cards."

Vince passed the thick, oversized deck to Nash. "Make me."

I knew that in the next moment, Tobin and Vince would be rolling around in the dirt, so I stepped forward and impersonated Winston's attitude after he'd thrown peanuts at the man. "Oh, we'll make you."

Vince looked at me, and then Tobin, and back to me. He took the cards from Nash and held them out to the old man. "Here, they're stupid, and I don't want 'em." As the old man reached for them, Vince threw them up in the air and they scattered.

Laughing, Vince and Nash ran off.

Tobin slapped my back. "Nice job. Real intimidating."

I grinned. "Just channeling my inner Winston."

We spent the next few minutes using our cell phone flashlights to help the old man locate and collect his cards. I looked at a few of the ones I picked up. The backs were featureless and yellow with age. The other sides depicted scenes from a time long past. One showed a knight with a sword in each hand; another had a dancing clown in a jester's outfit. A third depicted a witch with one eye staring at a crystal ball.

The old man counted the cards in his deck and smiled. "Thank you. Come inside," he said, pausing for a breath, "and I'll read the cards for you."

We followed him into the little tent, and unlike the others, this one seemed as small on the inside as it was on the outside. It smelled of mildew and old paper.

As the old man rounded a table and sat in a carved wooden chair, Tobin asked, "So what'd you tell Vince that made him so mad?"

He wheezed, and I realized it was a laugh. "That he would grow fat and go bald at an early age." He pulled back his hood. In the confines of the lantern-lit tent, his great age was evident. With long white hair and a beard, he looked like a wizard. Judging by how slow he walked, the uncertain way he moved, how he looked, I seriously thought he might be over a hundred years old.

As if he knew my thoughts, he said, "You wouldn't believe me if I told you how old I am." He shuffled the cards in a slow, clumsy fashion, dropping several. "Stupid arthritis." He picked up the fallen cards and added them to the deck. "Thanks again for helping me with those two." He nodded in the direction Vince and Nash had gone. "Sit down, sit down."

We sat across the table in spindly chairs.

"So you're a fortune-teller?" I asked.

The Oracle spoke in monotone, like it was an explanation he'd memorized. "The cards see what the future holds and then show the path to follow for the best of all outcomes."

"Cool," Tobin said. "I'll go first."

"Wait a minute," I said, taking off my backpack. I got out my art supplies. "You mind if I do a quick sketch of you?"

The Oracle looked surprised and then said, "Uh, sure."

"Thanks. Just do something you'd normally do."

The ancient man shuffled the cards again. "Interesting that you show up on Halloween night."

"Why's that?" I said, keeping my eyes on the charcoal and paper.

"Oh, this carnival is a lot like Halloween."

Tobin and I exchanged a glance, and then I turned back to my sketch. After a few minutes, I had the basic drawing, which I planned to return to later and finish from memory. I turned the pad and showed the Oracle.

"Oh, that's very good."

"He's going to be a famous artist someday," Tobin said.

"Hopefully," I added.

The Oracle looked at us for a long time, then he put down the deck and motioned us closer. He leaned over the table. "You helped me, so I'll help you." He looked to the tent entrance and then back to us. "I'm not like them."

"Huh?" Tobin said.

The ancient man's tongue licked parched lips. "Go! Get out of here!"

"Oracle." The three syllables of the word sounded like the lowest note of a tuba blown three times.

The old man jumped six inches in his chair. The slack expression of ancient age shifted into one of fear. He lifted his gaze to Big Guy at the tent flap. He hadn't entered, but he had inserted his head and shoulders.

"Hey, it's Big Guy," Tobin said. "How's it hanging?"

Ignoring Tobin, Big Guy asked, "What are you doing, Oracle?"

With a forced smile, the Oracle said, "I'm about to give these boys a reading, Falstaff."

Big Guy nodded. "On with it, then." He stayed and watched.

The Oracle spread the cards on the table and instructed us to pick three. "Put them in any order facedown in front of you." With shaking hands, he flipped Tobin's cards over and placed them side by side. He did the same with mine. "Ouch," the Oracle said, and held up his index finger, displaying a drop of blood. "Paper cut. A hazard in this line of work." As he spoke, he subtly placed his other hand on a card and covertly slid it off the table. He did it so stealthily I almost missed seeing him do it.

My first two cards matched Tobin's. One was a woman looking at her reflection in a pool of water. Totally absorbed by her mirror image, she didn't see the large, toothy creature in the water preparing to strike. The next identical card was the silhouette of two people gazing down a long, shadowy hallway.

The Oracle tapped Tobin's third card and said, "Hmmmm." It depicted the face of a young man peering out the barred windows of a dungeon or prison. The old man then tapped my third card and chuckled. It was a hawk with a shackle on one leg attached to a thin chain. The hawk was flying, and the picture captured the chain as it snapped.

"Oracle." Big Guy was still at the entry.

"Yes, yes." He turned his ancient eyes at us and spoke like it was a line he'd delivered hundreds of times. "Your futures are intertwined. Great things are ahead of you." He paused before adding, "If you first enter the House of Mystery and Mirrors."

"We're planning to hit it later," Tobin said.

The Oracle shook his head and said, "No. Now. The very next thing you do."

There was rustling behind us as the huge man pushed his way fully into the tent. Tobin and I stood. The tent went from cozy to claustrophobic with Big Guy taking up space.

The Oracle held out his hand to me, and we shook. "Thank you for coming."

"You're welcome."

He shook Tobin's hand. "Thank you for helping me with the bullies."

"No problem."

Big Guy held open the tent flap, and we slipped out under his arm. I paused and looked into the tent. Before the flap fell into place, I saw Big Guy grab the Oracle.

As we got to where the paper lanterns illuminated the path, I whispered, "He handed me something."

"Huh?"

"When he shook my hand, the Oracle passed me something."

Tobin glanced down at my closed right hand.

"He didn't want Big Guy to see it, so he slipped it to me."

Tobin pointed at a clump of people up ahead. "Over there."

Encircled by the crowd with a red lantern overhead, I opened my hand. It was one of the Oracle's cards, crumpled up. I flattened it, and it showed a skeletal figure in a hooded robe.

"Mean anything to you?" I asked.

"Nope."

I stared at it a moment longer and then flipped it over.

"Dude," Tobin muttered.

On the plain back of the card, the Oracle had used blood from his paper cut to give us a message: *Evil place. Leave.*

Dwelling on the Oracle's bloody message, we were quiet as we pushed through the crowds and got to the crossroads. I started to head straight toward the exit while Tobin turned left onto the one path we had yet to travel.

"Where are you going?" I asked.

"House of Mystery and Mirrors."

"But the Oracle's note."

We'd known each other almost our whole lives, so we'd developed a lot of knowledge about each other. For instance, I thought he could be reckless and too much of a daredevil. He, on the other hand, thought I was sometimes naive and too gullible.

His grin told me that's what he was thinking. "Come on, Zeus. It's all show."

I quoted the note. "Evil place. Leave."

"Yeah, and he also told us to go to the House of Mystery and Mirrors right away."

I said, "That was because Big Guy was watching us."

"It's just a carnival," Tobin said, enunciating each word as if to prove a point.

I shook my head and reached into my pocket to feel the Oracle's note. What did he mean by evil? How can a carnival be evil? Maybe some of the people who worked here were evil. But an entire carnival? Tobin was probably right; it was a bit of showmanship to make it that much more intriguing.

We went down the path for a time before noticing that things were getting weird. Up until then, the carnival had been jam-packed with people. But on the path leading to the House of Mystery and Mirrors, we were alone. The silence was profound.

Tobin looked back the way we'd come. "Uh, Zeus?"

The paper lanterns behind us extinguished one at a time, then the ones next to us, and finally all the lanterns in front of us. Several seconds later, two lights came on farther down the path. Both buzzed, brightening and dimming as if the electrical current was erratic. As we got closer, we saw that one was an old-fashioned streetlight. Fifty feet from that was the porch light of a house. An actual house that they'd somehow placed in the middle of the woods. How was that possible?

We mutely approached, stopping under the streetlight.

The two-story wooden farmhouse was old and painted black, and it looked like it would be full of ghosts. The roof was made of rusted metal. A porch encircled the house. The railing looked flimsy, like it would break at the slightest touch. Initially, the windows seemed dark, but now I saw dim illumination inside.

"Zeus." Tobin nodded toward the right side of the porch, where someone sat in the dark, pitching slowly back and forth in a creaking rocking chair.

The rocking stopped, and the figure stood. She stepped slowly toward the porch light. The Queen of the Carnival stood at the top of the porch stairs, smiling down at us.

"Zeus, Tobin, here you are. I have been waiting all night for you."

She wore a purple-and-silver ankle-length skirt. Her blouse was black, and over that, she wore an open half-jacket that matched her skirt. Her hair hung freely, and in it she wore an ornate diamond-and-silver comb.

Tobin leaned in and whispered, "How's she know our names?"

That was a good question.

The smile never left her lips as she descended the steps. She stopped at Tobin and took his hand in hers. After they shook, he stared down at his hand with a perplexed expression. When she took my hand, I knew why. Her skin was hot, like she had a fever. When she released me, it felt as if my hand were sunburned.

She turned and linked her arms through ours. Her perfume was a mix of caramel apples, cotton candy, and a hint of something that reminded me of a wild animal. With Tobin on one side of her and me on the other, we made our way to the house like Dorothy and her friends on the Yellow Brick Road. We ascended the porch stairs and stopped before the solid, dark-stained door. Still smiling, she pursed her lips and looked from Tobin to me. She opened the door and stepped inside. We followed a second later and found ourselves in a small room with well-worn furnishings and two small pictures on the walls.

"Gentlemen, welcome to the House of Mystery and Mirrors. It is a labyrinth of glass." The door slammed shut. "It is a maze of reflections." All around the room, mirrors rose up from the floor. "To get out, you have to success-fully work through the maze." Each mirror was two feet wide and rose to the ceiling. "I'll see you on the other side." She stepped between mirrors and vanished.

Some mirrors stood next to each other, while some were mounted at right angles, creating corridors. We had a choice of three leading from that room. And then we caught her reflections, some walking toward us, some away, some to the side. Again, she vanished, and a second later a half dozen mirrors reflected her face. She smiled, and all but one of her reflected faces vanished. The lone face paled to white flesh, and her skin drew taut. Black smudges appeared around her eyes, nostrils, and mouth. She opened her mouth wide, displaying a black tongue and throat, and then she was gone.

At first, we had a good time as we attempted the mirror maze. We chose the wrong hallway right off the bat and had to retrace our steps to the beginning and take another. That happened a lot. We tried mapping the maze in our heads. We'd think we'd found the way through the labyrinth, then WHAM, whoever was leading walked right into glass. We laughed hysterically when one of us hit a mirror. But the laughter lessened. After an hour, all humor was gone, replaced with growing anxiety.

We were constantly off-balance. Surrounded by mirrors, we were bombarded with reflections of reflections of reflections, producing countless Zeuses and Tobins. Each reflection got smaller and smaller until it seemed they vanished in the infinite distance. The hallways weren't very wide, so it had a closed-in effect, and with all those reflections, it seemed crowded. I doubted a claustrophobic person could handle it.

"Tobin, this isn't right."

"Yeah, I know." He stopped, and his multiple reflections shifted as he turned to me. "Like you said, we should have left when the Oracle told us to."

I pulled out my cell phone.

"Who are you calling?"

"I don't know. My parents, I guess." The screen remained black.

"What's the matter? No bars?"

"It's dead." I slipped it back into my pocket. "I charged it before I left the house."

Tobin took out his cell, tried to turn it on, and then showed me his black screen. "Something drained our batteries." Tobin put a hand on a mirror and then tapped it. "Do you have anything hard on you? Something that could break glass."

"What? Are you crazy? That's seven years bad luck," I said.

Tobin glared at me. "Forget your stupid superstitions." He gripped one end of the phone, holding it out lengthwise. "Get back." He reached back like he was preparing to pitch a baseball and then struck his phone hard against the glass. There was a thud, but he didn't come anywhere close to breaking the mirror. "Ouch!" he said, shaking his hand.

More time passed as we went through corridors of mirrors and halls of glass, retracing our steps and starting new routes. About this time, we started zoning out and stumbling through in a mental haze.

Tobin was the first to notice the mirrors had changed.

I blinked and looked around. No longer were they uniform and straight up and down. They leaned every which way and at differing angles. Some were thin and others fat. There were round mirrors, rectangles, squares, pentagons, hexagons, octagons, and more. Their frames differed as well. Some were framed with wood, others metal, some bamboo, some clay, some thin, some thick, and of every imaginable color. The only thing each mirror had in common was that they extended from the ceiling to the floor. Some were like fun house mirrors that distorted our appearance. In one, Tobin looked ten feet tall and thin as a rubber band. I stood next to him looking in another that made me appear three feet tall and six hundred pounds. On the other side of the corridor was a mirror that made Tobin's head twice as wide as his shoulders. The one next to that narrowed my torso to where

I'd have to wear two-inch-waist pants. Then we noticed something else. Because those mirrors faced each other, and provided infinite reflections, each reflection distorted the next, which further distorted the next, and so on. I looked at the smallest far distant reflection that I could make out, and it was a hideous creature, a misshapen and grotesque monster.

Besides the meandering maze, the floor began to rise in some places and descend in others. The ceiling did as well, but not parallel to the floor. Sometimes the ceiling would be as high as a cathedral's, and at times it was so low we had to get on our hands and knees. We started to get odd thoughts; the worst was that we were dead and condemned to a netherworld of mirrors. Things started to show up that weren't our reflections. We'd catch quick glimpses of movement.

"Did you see that?" Tobin asked.

"What?"

He pointed at a mirror of mist. "There."

For a split second I saw the silhouette of two shapes walking with their hands out in front of them. A pose I recognized from our own stumble through. The figures faded from view and then showed up several mirrors down. They disappeared from that mirror and appeared in the mirror right in front of us. Under our reflections, Vince and Nash faced us but were unaware that we were there.

"Hey!" I called.

"Vince! Nash!" Tobin yelled.

They didn't hear us, and we couldn't hear them. Crying, Vince silently banged on the glass with both of his fists. Nash had his phone in his hand and was stabbing at buttons. Frustrated, he threw the phone at the mirror, and it bounced off. Vince pointed in another direction, and they started off, disappearing.

We went on in the direction we'd been heading, blundering around in a dazed state. There was a cracking noise and then a buzzing much like the sound that accompanied the intermittent porch light and streetlight in front of the House of Mystery and Mirrors.

"Look!" Tobin said, excited.

Fifty feet away a neon sign lit up. In red letters it flashed EXIT.

Tobin was off in a second, running fast. He got to the sign before me. The mirror under it was enclosed in a gold frame and was both taller and wider than us, even as we stood side by side.

"This isn't any exit," Tobin grumbled in a low voice. His

face was a confusion of anger, frustration, and fear. He was unpredictable when he got like that.

I put a hand on his shoulder. "Tobin, are you all right?"

He brushed my hand away. "I'm sick of this."

"I know; me too."

His lips twisted into a sneer. Curling both hands into fists, he lifted them over his head and brought them down toward the mirror while roaring in anger. There was no impact against glass. His fists continued through, and he tripped forward, the upper half of his body disappearing into the mirror. I caught him around the waist and pulled him back out.

Tentatively, I put my hand forward and encountered no glass. When my hand passed through the frame, it encountered cooler, drier air.

Tobin poked a hand back through and, with wide-eyed astonishment, said, "This mirror, we can go through it. I saw a hallway in a house."

We stood before it a long time.

I said, "It's a door. No, wait, more like a portal."

"Mysterious passageway."

"Threshold."

"Gateway."

Turning to him, I said, "Whatever you want to call it, it's not right."

Tobin pushed his head through the frame. "Smells like mildew and dust." He pulled his head back out. "Let's go through."

I thought about it, swallowed, and pushed my head through the mirrored surface. I studied what I saw and withdrew. "On the other side, that could be the inside of the House of Mystery and Mirrors without the maze. Maybe that's how we get out. We go through and explore until we find a door out."

Tobin pulled me into a bear hug. "Zeus, I think we made it." Releasing me, he stepped through the mirror.

I joined him, and we started down the dimly lit hallway.

My voice trembled as I spoke about Tobin and me and our journey in the mirrors. Jana and I had picked a spot further along in my story to take a break and get to some of our prerecorded tales, but talking about it really disturbed me, to the point that my hands were shaking. It's not the first time that's happened. I'd gotten the shakes more than once when talking with Jana about Carnival Nocturne. She thinks I have post-traumatic stress disorder. She even looked up the symptoms. Nightmares; feeling distant from other people; what they call hypervigilance, trying to be ready for any kind of threat;

insomnia; flashbacks to being in the mirrors. Yeah, I got those. Another symptom is having negative thoughts about myself. Mainly because I got out and Tobin didn't. That's something called survivor's guilt.

When Jana saw I had to stop, she brought up our theme song. She killed our mics and pulled one of her headphones from her ear. I did the same.

I swallowed and said, "Sorry. I don't think I can go on right now."

"Drink some water, then come back and intro our first group of stories."

I followed her advice, took some deep breaths, and nodded at her. She brought up the levels on my mic.

"I'm Zeus, and you're listening to the podcast *Odd Occurrences*. I'm going to pause right now in the telling of my own personal odd occurrence so that we can share with you some of the stories submitted by listeners." I picked up my clipboard and saw that I still shook a little. "We have quite the collection to share with you this Halloween night." I nodded to Jana.

She consulted her own clipboard. "First up is something I've always wanted to try—an escape room."

"We'll follow that up with why you should never open

your doors to strangers, as an urban legend proves to be more of an urban reality," I said.

"An *Odd Occurrences* listener will share what happened to his grandmother when she was a little girl in war-torn Europe."

"We'll show you how fairy tales are very much like nightmares."

"And an odd occurrence that starts in the laboratory of a mad scientist," Jana said.

"After those, I'll pick up my story of the House of Mystery and Mirrors. As you listen to these upcoming accounts, ask yourself, how would you handle things, if you found yourself trapped in an odd occurrence?"

Jana brought up our theme song for a few beats and then started our first prerecorded story.

- CHAPTER 3 -
THE ESCAPE (OR ELSE) ROOM

"Awesome room," Aubrey said. He spun, taking it in. He was already six feet, two inches tall even though he was still in middle school. His hair was a nest of loose black curls. A third of his face was scar tissue several shades lighter than his normally dark complexion. He'd been mauled by a neighbor's dog when he was four.

"It sure looks like a Victorian-era study." Kadien read all the time and was really smart. He knew stuff like that. He was small with neatly trimmed black hair. "Whaddya think, Izzy?"

"I think we're gonna escape in record time."

It all started with a bike ride Izzy took the other day. A

few miles out of town, she saw a narrow gravel driveway with a small sign beside it that said COMING SOON, ESCAPE (OR ELSE) ROOM. She walked her bike up the driveway to a big, gray, square building, kind of like a warehouse. There were no windows, and only one door at the front. She continued across the parking lot and read a piece of paper taped to the door: OPENING SOON.

She'd taken about a dozen steps back toward the driveway when someone said, "Can I help you, young lady?"

Izzy turned and saw a man in a mustard-colored suit and red bow tie standing in the open door. He had shoulder-length black hair and a million wrinkles on his face.

"I was riding by and saw your sign. Thought I'd check it out."

"We open next month. I do hope you'll come back and bring friends."

"Sure." Glancing at the building, she said, "It's big."

The man scrutinized her and then snapped his fingers. "You know, next week we're beta testing."

"What's that?"

"We'll have people try out our *Escape (or Else) Room* to make sure we have all the bugs worked out before we open it to the public. Would you like to give it a go, free of charge?"

Izzy couldn't have smiled any wider. "You bet!"

The man reached into his jacket pocket and pulled out a piece of paper. "What's your name?"

"Izzy Baxter."

The man scribbled the information. "Good, good. I'm the game master. Bring friends on Wednesday, at, oh, say, four in the afternoon."

"We'll be here."

"Oh, and a little advice. Don't tell your parents you're coming. In my experience, they freak out when they hear the term *beta testing* and don't allow their little darlings to participate."

Izzy shrugged. "Okay."

And that's how they ended up in what Kadien called a Victorian-era study. Izzy pulled her long brown hair into a ponytail and secured it with a scrunchie. "All right, let's get this show on the road."

"Greetings, escapees," the game master's voice came through hidden speakers. "Today will be a three-room literary challenge. Each room will be based on a famous book or story. You have a one-hour time limit to make it through the first room, forty-five minutes for the second, and thirty minutes for the third."

"Whoa, wait a minute," Kadien said. "That means if we use up all the time limits, we won't get out until after six. My family has dinner at six. I'll be grounded if I'm late."

"Then you better be faster than the time limits," the game master said. "The rules are simple. There are hidden clues that will help you escape this room. At the beginning of each room, I will give you a clue to get you started."

"I can't be late for dinner. Maybe you better let me out."

"Your first is the *Hound of the Baskervilles* room."

As worried as Kadien was about being late for dinner, his face lit up. "That's a famous Sherlock Holmes story. This must be Sherlock Holmes's study from 221B Baker Street."

"Correct," the game master said. "And your first clue for this room is this: *If at first you don't succeed, die and die again.*"

Kadien looked worried again. "But—"

Izzy put an arm over Kadien's shoulders. "We'll escape early so you won't get in trouble."

Kadien nodded. "*The Hound of the Baskervilles* is about this giant ghost dog that haunts the moors and kills members of the Baskerville family."

"Ugh," Aubrey said. Because of his canine attack years earlier, he had an overwhelming fear of dogs.

They took stock of the room, which included book-cases on all the walls, containing hundreds of books.

"I wonder why we had to hand over our cell phones?" Aubrey said.

Izzy shrugged. "Maybe so we can't go online to get help for any hard clues."

"The room is cool and all," Kadien said, then dropped his voice to a whisper, "but I don't like the game master."

Aubrey nodded. "And what was that stuff about our darkest fears?"

When they'd first arrived, Izzy introduced her friends to the game master.

The game master took Aubrey's hand and stared at him. "Let me see what I can learn about you from your eyes. Hmmm, your darkest fear is being torn to pieces by a mad dog."

Aubrey gasped. "What? How did you—"

The game master next shook Kadien's hand and said, "You lean toward claustrophobia—a fear of being trapped in small spaces."

Kadien stood with an open mouth. He was so claustro-phobic that he wouldn't play hide-and-seek because all the good hiding spaces are usually little hidey-holes.

The game master turned to Izzy and held out his hand.

She reluctantly took it. "And Izzy. Interesting. A fear of water, is it?"

"Not all water," she said defensively.

"Just if the water is over her head," Kadien said.

"She won't even go in a swimming pool," Aubrey added.

The game master had given Izzy a yellow-tooth smile and released her hand.

In their first challenge, a fire crackled in the fireplace. Two crossed swords were mounted over the mantel. There was a large, old-fashioned desk cluttered with papers and antique office supplies. A glass case contained a collection of exotic knives and daggers. Numerous framed pictures, landscapes and portraits, hung on the walls, along with three animal-head trophies. A doll sat in a chair in the corner. It seemed out of place because it was missing an eye and was so dirty. Kadien stood next to a violin on a stand, its bow next to it. He plucked a string a couple of times.

Aubrey asked, "What about the clue the game master gave us? *If at first you don't succeed, die and die again?*"

Izzy had an idea. "Look for things that can kill."

They started with the mounted animal heads, a lion, a bear, and a boar. Aubrey and Izzy pulled over a couple of chairs to stand on and looked in their mouths and ears and felt along the fur.

"This could kill someone." Kadien held up a pointy letter opener he got from the desktop.

"Look around where you found it," Izzy said.

Aubrey peered into the case with the knife collection. "There are a dozen ways to die in here, but it's locked."

What he said struck a chord with Izzy. "'There are a dozen ways to die in here,'" she repeated. "Hey, maybe the clue was specific about the number of ways to die. *If at first you don't succeed, die and die again.* Did that mean two deaths?" She looked around before pointing to the two crossed swords over the fireplace mantel. "There!" She grabbed a chair, pulled it in front of the fireplace, and stood on it. Izzy took one of the swords off the wall and handed it to Aubrey. She got the other one and jumped from the chair.

"There's writing," Aubrey said, looking at his sword.

Words had been etched into the blades. "*Feeling hungry? Don't eat mud,*" Izzy read out loud.

Aubrey looked at his sword. "Mine says, *Take a bite and drink some blood.*"

Izzy checked her watch. "We found the second clue in just under ten minutes. Let's figure this one out and get out of here way early."

That turned out to be wishful thinking. They spent the

next thirty-plus minutes wandering the study, rummaging desk drawers, looking for secret hiding spaces. They wasted time with several still-life paintings of food. Then they turned their attention to finding anything that had to do with blood, and that led to hunting down everything that was red. Kadien focused his attention on the books in the bookcases. Another five minutes passed.

"Aha!" Kadien shouted.

"Aha, what?" Izzy asked.

Kadien held up a thick, old leather-bound book. "*Dracula* by Bram Stoker. The greatest vampire story ever."

"Ohhhhhh," Izzy said, feeling dumb. *"Feeling hungry? Don't eat mud. Take a bite and drink some blood."*

Kadien opened the book. "Check this out." A small square had been cut out of the middle of the pages, about two inches deep. And inside the hole was an antique key.

"The locked drawer," Aubrey said.

Izzy took out the key and ran to the desk. The key fit. She unlocked the drawer, pulled it out, and saw it was empty, save for a scrap of paper, which read, *To leave the room, you don't need keys. All you need is to play high Cs.*

"Thankfully my parents make me take violin lessons," Kadien said, and hurried to the violin. He took it and the bow from the stand, tucked the violin under his chin, and rested the bow across a string. He pressed a string to the neck with a left-hand finger. "Prepare to leave the room." With a flourish, he pulled the bow across the string, and a note sang out. "That's the highest C on a violin." Nothing happened.

"It says you have to play high Cs, plural," Aubrey said.

Kadien nodded and started running the bow back and forth over the string. Still nothing.

The game master's voice filled the room. "Five minutes left. Would you like a hint?"

"Yes," Aubrey said.

"No," Izzy said at the same time. She turned away in frustration and muttered, "*To leave the room, you don't need keys. All you need is to play high Cs.*" She repeated it over and over as she ran around the room.

"Three minutes left until *or else*. Would you like a hint?"

"Izzy, come on," Aubrey said.

She sighed in defeat. "Fine."

"We'll take a hint," Aubrey said.

The game master spoke slowly, enunciating each word. "*Don't be sad, it's just a game. What you seek is in a frame.*"

A painting caught Izzy's eye. It depicted a ship with tall masts on storm-tossed seas. Four straight lines ran parallel to each other, angling up from the bottom left corner to the top right corner. Moving closer, she saw that the lines were taut steel wires—or strings, as in guitar strings.

"Guys," she said. "Playing the high Cs means playing the painting of the high seas." She strummed the strings. The room filled with chamber music.

"Congratulations," the game master's voice boomed over the music. "You have completed the first room. However, because you asked for a hint, there will be a penalty."

"What? That's not fair. You didn't say anything about penalties," Aubrey called out.

"What's the penalty?" Izzy figured he'd deduct time from the limit for the next room.

"You have to play a round of musical squares. Please note the gold tile squares on the floor in the middle of the room." Almost all the tiles were faded red with blue designs. But there were three big golden tiles set in a triangle pattern. "While the music plays, please walk around those tiles. When the music stops, you must hop onto the nearest gold tile."

Izzy looked at the others and shrugged. They went to the gold tiles and started walking from one to the next. After they'd been around about a half dozen times, the chamber music stopped. Laughing, they all jumped on whatever gold tile was closest. Izzy looked at Aubrey, who grinned at her. In the next second, his tile dropped, and he fell through the floor. From below came low growls of large animals. Aubrey screamed, and the gold tile swung back up into place. It had been hinged, and now that it was closed, Izzy couldn't hear anything from below. She and Kadien stared numbly at where Aubrey had been standing.

There was a loud click, and one of the bookcases swung open, revealing a doorway.

"Please proceed to the next room," the game master said.

It took a few seconds, but Izzy found her voice. "Wait! Where's Aubrey?"

"Losing him was your penalty," the game master said. And then, in a matter-of-fact tone, he added, "The *or else* got him."

"We heard growls," Izzy said.

The game master seemed to gloat as he said, "Well, it is the *Hound of the Baskervilles* room."

Stunned, Izzy stumbled toward the open door, but she stopped when she realized Kadien wasn't following. He stared open-mouthed at where Aubrey had fallen through the floor, and he was silently crying.

She went and took him by his arms. "Kadien." He didn't respond. "Kadien, look at me."

His eyes lifted to her face, tears rolling down both cheeks. "Aubrey's gone, Izzy. Is he dead?"

"No." Izzy shook her head fiercely. "No way. He just lost and got booted from the escape room. He's probably outside right now, waiting for us to finish."

Kadien's eyes lit up. "You really think so?"

"I'm positive," she said, but in her mind, she thought, *I hope so, I really do.*

Kadien wiped away the tears, and they went through the open door into a hallway. Other than buzzing incandescent tube lights overhead, the walls, floor, and ceiling were featureless. The final stretch of the hallway was shrouded in dark. A light switched on, and they saw oversized red and brown bricks, thick mortar between each. The brick wall swung in, revealing the next room.

Murky, with shadows everywhere, the room was inadequately lit by four torches mounted in sconces. The same red and brown bricks were used in the floors, ceiling, and walls. Water leaked in with the repetitive sound of drops falling from the ceiling into puddles on the floor. Small, shadowed figures skittered along the base of the walls.

"Rats," Kadien said in disgust.

Countless alcoves, recesses, nooks, and crannies were layered in varying degrees of shadow.

Kadien walked up to an alcove and peered in. "Oh no."

"What?"

"I think I know what this room is." Just to the side of the alcove were three huge wooden barrels on their sides, one stacked on top of the other two. "Wine casks." Scattered around the floor were what looked like human bones, including a skull. "Look." Kadien pointed into the alcove, which was about the size of a small closet. Two chains ending in shackles were attached to an iron ring mounted to the wall. "I think we're in the catacombs from the Edgar Allan Poe story 'The Cask of Amontillado.' If I remember it correctly, this guy named Montresor lures another man, Fortunato, into the catacombs under his house with the promise of tasting an expensive Spanish sherry called amontillado."

"What's sherry?"

"It's like wine," Kadien said. He stepped into the recess and handled one of the chains. "Anyway, Montresor thinks that Fortunato insulted him sometime in the past, so Montresor gets revenge by chaining Fortunato to a wall in one of the little nooks in the catacombs, and then he bricks him inside and leaves."

Izzy studied the shackles and involuntarily shivered. She called out, "Hey, we're here. What's the first clue?"

Like in Sherlock Holmes's study, the game master's voice was piped in. *"To this room you have been led. The clue you seek is in his head.* You have forty-five minutes."

"That's easy." Izzy strode over to the skull and picked it up. She turned it over, and a piece of paper was inside.

"What's it say?" Kadien asked.

Izzy read out loud. *"Some might say it's all mysterious. Others would say it's all just humerus.* Ha! He misspelled *humorous.*"

Kadien's eyes widened. "How'd he spell it?"

"H-u-m-e-r-u-s."

"He didn't misspell it. The humerus is a type of bone." Kadien pointed at his arm. "The bone that runs from the shoulder to the elbow." He started picking up bones and looking them over. "Look for a bone that is long, shoulder to elbow."

It took only a minute for Kadien to find it. "Got it." He held it above his head.

Izzy high-fived his free hand. "This room is easy." Taking the bone, she saw there were letters burned into it. *"Time runs down and things are starker, the key to leave is to make it darker.* What's that mean?"

Kadien thought a moment. "I don't know. Maybe the next clue is where it's dark."

"It's dark everywhere down here." They spent the next half hour poking into murky nooks, crannies, alcoves, and recesses. Izzy pulled a torch from a sconce and went deeper into the catacombs, which seemed to go on forever, but they figured any clue would be hidden in the general area they'd been in. The minutes seemed to fly by, and with each passing second, their anxiety rose. It sounded like they were chanting as they both repeated the clue over and over, in the hope that the next recitation would make it clear.

And then they heard what they'd been dreading, the game master's voice. "Five minutes until *or else*. Do you want a hint?"

They looked at each other. The fear Izzy saw on Kadien's face was reflected on her own. They'd need a hint to escape, but if they took a hint, there'd be an *or else* penalty.

"*Time runs down and things are starker, the key to leave is to make it darker*," Izzy said for the umpteenth time. "Come on, think."

It seemed as if only a second had passed when they heard, "Three minutes until *or else*. Would you like a hint?"

"No," Izzy screamed.

She dashed in and out of shadows, running the torch up and down the bricks, looking for what she couldn't find.

"Two minutes until *or else*. Would you like a hint?"

Izzy didn't bother to answer him.

"Izzy?" Kadien said.

She stood frozen until the game master said, "One minute until *or else*. Do you want a hint?"

Izzy couldn't answer, because they did need that hint, but at what cost?

"Yes!" Kadien shouted in a shrill voice. "Give us the hint!"

"Very well. *Be careful that you don't get scorched, getting the key from the torch.*"

Stunned, Izzy stared at the torch in her hand.

"Thirty seconds until *or else*."

"Izzy!" Kadien shouted.

Izzy ran to a puddle, turned the torch upside down, and plunged it into the water. The fire extinguished with a hiss. Though three torches still burned, the loss of one dimmed the room considerably. Mounted in the top of the torch where the fire had burned was an antique key.

Quenching in the water had cooled it enough that Izzy could hold it, and she plucked it from the torch.

"With three seconds to spare, you have succeeded," the game master said. "Of course, there is the matter of a penalty for the hint. Rock, paper, or scissors?"

Totally confused, Izzy blurted out, "What?"

"Both of you choose rock, or paper, or scissors."

Izzy and Kadien stared at each other, their eyes wide.

"If no one chooses, you both suffer a penalty, and the session is over…permanently."

"Rock," Kadien shouted at the same time Izzy yelled, "Scissors."

"Excellent. You aren't going against each other, but what is in those wine casks. Izzy, go select one of the barrels. If it contains a rock, scissors loses. If it contains paper, rock loses. If it contains scissors, it defeats neither scissors nor rock, and you will both move on to the final room. Go on, Izzy."

Izzy touched each barrel, one on top of two, and finally said, "The top one."

"Open it," the game master said.

There was a wooden handle at the end of each barrel. Izzy grabbed the one she'd chosen and pulled it open.

"Be scissors, please be scissors, please," Kadien muttered.

Izzy reached in and looked at Kadien.

"What? What is it?"

Silently, with tears starting down her cheeks, she removed a sheet of paper.

The flames on the other torches sputtered, got smaller, and finally went out. They were in total darkness in the catacombs.

"Izzy?" Kadien said, and a second later he shrieked. The sounds Izzy heard between Kadien's screams were surreal. There was one metallic snap, followed by another. Then other sounds started; a long scrape and what sounded like two rocks knocking together. Scrape—knock, scrape—knock, scrape—knock. It came again, and again, and again. Izzy tried to get to Kadien, but something, fear maybe, held her in place. The sounds increased in tempo, getting faster and faster until it sounded like someone riffling cards. By then, Kadien had stopped screaming. Flames sprouted in the torches and grew. The little alcove next to the wine casks and bones had been bricked over, with one rectangular hole remaining. Wet mortar had been troweled around the edges of the opening.

Izzy grabbed a lit torch and held it up to the hole. "Kadien?" She could just see him in that tiny space. The shackles were locked around his wrists. He was in shock. A brick rose into view on the other side and slid into the hole, sealing Kadien inside.

Izzy lay on a sandy beach gripping a pair of swimming goggles, the ocean lapping at the shore. There were palm trees behind her, and the songs of exotic birds filled the air. The game master had informed her earlier that this was the *Robinson Crusoe* room, based on the book about the man who was marooned for years on a desert island. Izzy found three clues, one after the other, and the third clue was the one that had her shivering under a tropical sun.

She asked a question. "Who are you?"

The voice came in over the waves. "I am the game master."

"Who are you really?"

The game master was silent so long she thought he was ignoring her question. But then he spoke. "I can tell you many of the names I've had throughout my existence. Norsemen called me Loki. The Greeks called me Pan. The Japanese called me Kitsune. In Bulgaria, I was Sly Peter, while the Hopi nation called me Kokopelli. According to West Africans, I was Anansi."

"Why are you doing this?" Izzy asked, trying not to cry.

"Because it is my nature. I am a trickster."

Impossible, but no more impossible than being on an island, surrounded by ocean, with the sun overhead, while stuck inside an escape room. "Loki? Pan? So you're a god?"

"I have been called such, but no. What I am is not human. What I am is immortal. Deception is my character. By the way, you have less than ten minutes until the *or else*. Are you stumped? Do you need a hint?"

"I know what I have to do."

"Ahh, your fear of water is stopping you." The last clue was *Descend the depths to Neptune's room, the key is in the watery gloom.* "Perhaps you need inspiration."

The sky went black. A thin line of white separated the sky into two equal halves. And in one Izzy saw Aubrey; in the other she saw Kadien. It was like she was looking at the biggest security monitor in the world. Both of her friends were petrified with fear. Aubrey huddled in the corner of a room. Gigantic dogs the size of small horses were secured with thick iron chains attached to spiked collars. Their muzzles were coated in foam as they snarled and lunged at Aubrey, who was just out of reach. On the other side of the sky, Kadien was shackled in the tiny space that had been bricked up in the catacombs. His wide eyes looked blindly one way and then the other. He trembled violently.

"Let them go!" Izzy screamed, jumping to her feet.

"It's up to you, not me."

"What do you mean?"

"I mean, if you escape this room in time, I will release your friends. If you don't escape, well then, you'll face your own *or else*, and theirs will become permanent."

Izzy felt energized. "You mean there's a chance we can all escape?"

"There's always a chance—until there's not."

She slipped the goggles over her eyes and ran toward the waves. She'd had a fear of water her whole life. Just looking at a swimming pool could make her sick. She didn't even know how to swim. *No,* she told herself. *Don't think about it. Just do it.* She pushed into the water, struggling as the current tried to push her back to shore. She fought through until she was waist-deep and then chest-deep. A wave broke on her face, and she sucked in salt water, wasting a whole minute coughing it back up.

At neck-deep, Izzy took a deep breath and put her face

in the water. She was on a ledge, and just past that was a dark abyss. Next to her was a basketball-sized rock. She took a moment to suck in as much air as possible, then she ducked beneath the surface, picked up the rock, and stepped off the ledge. She descended to the depths, a slow plummet into water deep enough that the pressure made her eardrums feel like they were being pierced with needles.

Izzy hit bottom. Visibility down there was only about twenty feet. Spectral shapes of large fish, bigger than her, would appear out of the gloom and then vanish back in. At her feet, a pirate's treasure chest rested in the silty sand. She opened the chest with one hand and lifted the lid. The only thing inside was a key, and she grabbed it. A shark appeared from the murkiness and swam right at her, its tail slashing from side to side. She held up the key and closed her eyes.

When she opened them again, she was curled on her side. It was night, and she sucked in air.

"Izzy?"

Aubrey and Kadien were in front of her, both looking as dazed as she felt.

"Why are you wet?" Kadien asked.

Izzy was soaked. They were outside where the *Escape*

(or Else) Room building had been. It was no longer there. It had been replaced by a grassy field.

There was the chirp of a ringtone, and Kadien pulled out his phone. He checked the caller ID. "My parents. I am so dead."

Izzy looked back at where the building had once been. "No. No, you're not. You're alive. We all are." Izzy smiled at her friends. "We escaped."

CHAPTER 4

BLACK-EYED KIDS

"I ran," Noah said at the beginning of the recording. "Like a coward. But if I hadn't, there wouldn't be anyone to tell you this odd occurrence...."

"Ahh, this is the life, the babysitting part of the evening is over, we can stay up late and watch scary movies, and we've got a well-stocked refrigerator," Noah said, falling onto the sofa with a half-eaten ice-cream sandwich in his hand. He was a short, stocky kid, and he wore purple pajama bottoms with a white T-shirt. His free hand rested on the sofa, and he pulled something from between two cushions. "Yuck." He held up an old, one-eyed doll with brown hair. "Doesn't your sister ever clean her toys?" he asked, and tossed it to the floor.

Dylan shrugged and kicked back in his dad's lounge chair, holding a remote and looking at the options on their flat-screen TV. "So, what do you think? Zombies, aliens, or ghosts?" Dylan was four inches taller than his best friend, had shaggy blond hair, and lounged in his sweatpants and black sleeveless T-shirt.

"Ummm, ghosts. Yeah, definitely ghosts."

Dylan's parents were spending the night at what they called a charming little bed-and-breakfast a couple of hours up the coast. For the first time, they told Dylan he was old enough for the responsibility and left him in charge. The best part was they would pay him for it. They were fine with Noah staying over, too. Dylan's mom always said he was part of the family.

"Ghosts it is. Let's see, gothic ghost story, modern ghost story, or Japanese ghost story?"

"Japanese," Noah said through a mouthful of ice-cream sandwich. He held up a hand while he finished chewing. "Did you know the Japanese call ghosts yūrei? *Yū* means 'faint,' and *rei* means 'spirit.' The onryō yūrei are the worst; they can kill you. *Onryō* means 'vengeful spirit.'"

Dylan chuckled at his friend. He was a vault of knowledge

when it came to the supernatural, especially folklore and urban legends. That night, he'd already talked about the vetala, zombies in Hindu mythology. Then about Gilles Garnier, a Frenchman in the sixteenth century who claimed to have an ointment that would turn him into a wolf. How he was burned at the stake after eating a bunch of kids. And then Noah went on about the boo hag, which Dylan had to admit was pretty cool. The boo hag was a witch in Gullah folklore who removed her skin every night, which allowed her to fly and hunt for victims.

The aroma of fresh-popped popcorn wafted through the living room as they settled in to watch a movie about a haunted house in Japan. It got intense, and they leaned forward as the main character made her way down a dark hallway, unaware of the ghost girl moving jerkily behind her.

Tap, tap, tap.

They exchanged glances.

"Did you hear that?" Noah asked.

"I heard something." Dylan grabbed the remote from the coffee table and paused the movie.

Tap, tap, tap.

"There it is again."

"I think someone's at the door," Dylan said.

"After midnight?" Noah questioned. "And why not use the doorbell?"

Tap, tap, tap.

Dylan slowly got up and moved across the room to the door; Noah was right behind him.

Tap, tap, tap.

Dylan switched on the porch light and looked out a narrow window in the door that was at face height. "I don't see anybody."

Tap, tap, tap.

Dylan backed up, stepping on Noah's foot.

"Ouch. Watch it."

Tap, tap, tap.

Dylan stepped up to the door and put his face right at the window and looked down. "What the..."

"What the...what?"

"It's a couple of kids."

"Kids?" Noah put his head next to Dylan's and looked down. His guts twisted when he realized what he was looking at.

A boy, maybe ten years old, stood on the front stoop. A younger girl was next to him, holding his hand.

Dylan reached for the doorknob.

"What are you doing?" Noah blurted out.

"Opening the door. It's a couple of kids."

Noah grabbed Dylan's wrist and stopped him. "At this time of night? And did you notice their clothes?"

Dylan jerked his hand free. "No, why?" He peeked out at them again.

"They're old; I mean the clothing style."

"What are you talking about?"

Tap, tap, tap.

Noah joined Dylan at the window. "See? He's wearing that old-fashioned shirt made out of some thick material."

"So?"

Noah pushed his index finger against the glass to point. "Look, suspenders. I mean, come on, suspenders? And look at her in that old-fashioned dress. And you know what that is over the dress? That's an apron. What kind of kid wears an apron these days?"

Dylan smirked at him. "An apron? How diabolical."

"I'm serious."

Tap, tap, tap. "*Helloooo. Can you help us? We're lost,*" the boy spoke in a singsong rhythm.

Dylan reached for the knob again, but Noah's hand got there first and held it firm. "Did you see their faces?" he spoke slowly, emphasizing each word.

"What? No. They're looking down. Now get out of the

way." Dylan pushed Noah's hand from the doorknob and opened the door.

Immediately they were hit with a feeling of dread. Both of them. It was like watching a scary movie and someone was about to go into a basement, not knowing that the killer was waiting down there. It was the same kind of feeling multiplied a hundred times over. When the fear struck Dylan, he stopped opening the door. It was only cracked several inches.

"What..." Dylan's voice was hoarse. He swallowed and said, "What do you want?"

The boy spoke too softly to hear. Noah stepped next to Dylan and peered out. Both children were still looking down, and both had on worn, lace-up boots. The boy's hairstyle looked as if someone had plopped a bowl on his head and cut it evenly across. The girl's straw-colored hair was in pigtails, with two worn bits of fabric serving as bows at the ends.

"What'd you say?" Dylan asked.

"*Can we come in? It's coooold. We're lost. My sister has to use the bathroom.*"

Dylan was quiet a moment and then said, "Well, I suppose you can—"

"Wait!" Noah shouted, and then put his foot behind

the door so Dylan couldn't open it any more than it was. He spoke to the kids, "Look at us."

The two kids stood without moving.

"We won't let you in if you don't look at us," he said.

Moving at the same time, the boy and girl lifted their heads.

Dylan and Noah screamed. The porch light flickered and went out. Noah shoved Dylan out of the way, closed the door, and turned the dead bolt lock.

Dylan stood numbly, staring at nothing. "Did you—did you see their eyes?"

Noah nodded and muttered, "B.E.K.s."

Dylan's face was drained of color. "B.E.K.s? What's that?"

"Black-eyed kids."

"Yeah, yeah, their eyes were black." Dylan peeked out the window again, but it was too dark to see. He paced a few steps, turned, and paced back. "Their eyes, what should be the whites, what should be the colored part, all black."

Noah was too shaken to stand, and he placed his back against the door and slid down to sit on the foyer floor. "Oh, this is bad, I mean really bad. Black-eyed kids? Here? In our town? At your house?"

"Are they sick, is that it? Are they—wait a minute. Is this one of those weird things you know all about, like shadow figures and the Fresno nightcrawlers?" Dylan asked.

Noah hugged his knees and stared straight out. "Yes, an urban legend kind of thing that's been around for a few decades, and—"

Tap, tap, tap.

"*Let us iiiiin. It's coooold.*"

That inspired Noah to get to his feet and back away from the door. "Don't let them in."

Dylan stared at the door and whispered, "What would happen if we did?"

Noah got behind Dylan and peeked around him at the door. "That's just it. No one knows."

"Huh?"

"No one knows what happens, because all the stories come from people who *didn't* let them in. Get it? No one knows what happens to people who let them in because people who do aren't around anymore to tell anyone what happened."

"Oh." Dylan went to the coffee table and picked up the flashlight. Back at the door, he clicked it on and aimed it down through the window. "They're not there anymore." He looked at Noah with a hopeful smile. "They left."

"No. They don't just leave, not right away."

Tap, tap, tap.

They turned to the living room.

"The window," Dylan whispered. "What do these urban legends say about black-eyed kids?"

"Creepy stuff. They show up late at night. They're dressed as if they're from another time. They want to come in and have all sorts of reasons you should let them. I mean, who's going to tell little kids to go away late at night? But when people open their door, they're overcome with fear. The B.E.K.s usually come in twos. Their age can be anywhere from a toddler to about sixteen."

Tap, tap, tap.

Dylan stared at the living room window. He turned to Noah, fear evident in his eyes. He swallowed and said, "I can't believe they're out there. What else do you know?"

Noah gazed down as he thought. "Ummm, well, there are two main theories. Some people think it's a fairly new phenomenon. The first documented case was in Abilene, Texas. A reporter claimed he was sitting in his car late at night, heard a knock on his window, and turned to see two B.E.K.s. They told him they needed a ride home. He almost unlocked the doors but stopped when he was overcome with powerful dread."

"Yeah, definitely felt that. Dread with a capital *D*," Dylan said, and visibly shivered.

"They kept banging on his window and pleading with him. Finally, he drove off. Other people think the phenomenon goes back much further."

Tap, tap, tap.

"Pleeeeeeeease, let us innnnn."

Noah yelped. "They're at the front door again."

Dylan asked, "What did you mean when you said some people think the phenomenon goes further back?"

It took a moment for Noah to shake off the heebie-jeebies. "Um, yeah. Some think there are references to them going back a long way. There's an old folk song that originated in the Appalachian Mountains in the eighteen hundreds. I can't remember the lyrics exactly, but it's along these lines:

"'Let us in,' they said, the little boy and girl.

"Late at night, at my door, I'm ignorant of my peril.

"I should have locked them out, instead of what I did,

"It's too late, I let them in, a pair of black-eyed kids.

"A Native American group, the Iroquois, believed in an evil presence called the Otkon. If this evil caught Iroquois children in the woods, it would take over their bodies."

"Like a possession?" Dylan asked.

"Could be. When these kids came back from the woods, they had black eyes and pale skin. They attempted to enter their homes, which for the Iroquois were longhouses that a dozen or more families would share. They believed these children infected by Otkon's evil wanted to destroy the village and infect them all with Otkon."

"So these two kids intend to either make us like them or destroy us?" Dylan asked in a panicked tone.

"Yes. No. Maybe. No one really knows."

"What do we do?" Dylan asked.

"Don't let them in."

"I mean, besides that. Wait, I know." Dylan pulled his cell phone from a pocket and pressed some buttons.

"Who are you calling?"

"The police, who else?"

"Yeah, good idea."

Dylan tapped the Speaker button and held the phone out.

There was a click, followed by a woman's voice. "9-1-1, what's your emergency?"

"Yes, hi. Yeah, I think it's an emergency. My parents are out of town, and someone is trying to get into our house."

"A burglar is attempting to enter your home?"

"What? No, not a burglar."

"You have a prowler?"

"Not a prowler, either," Dylan said.

The dispatcher said, "Who's trying to get into your house, young man?"

"It's a couple of kids."

"Could you repeat that, please?"

"Kids, young kids."

Noah lost his patience, grabbed Dylan's hand, and pulled the phone toward him. "They've got black eyes."

"Are you saying the children have been beaten? Are bruised with black eyes?"

"Not that," Noah yelled. "You know, the urban legend about black-eyed kids. No one knows what they are: vampires, ghosts, zombies. They come late at night, and you can't let them in, otherwise—"

"Calling 9-1-1 isn't a joke," the dispatcher said sharply. "Call again and you'll see how much trouble you can get into."

"Hello? Hello?" Dylan looked up from the phone. "She hung up."

Tap, tap, tap.

The tapping came from another location. They looked at each other and then ran toward the sound. Both knew they weren't being brave and rushing toward danger; it's just that they'd feel safer if they knew where the B.E.K.s were. The lights were out in the kitchen.

The boys stopped at the side of the refrigerator, and Dylan peeked around it and whispered, "Look at the back door."

Noah leaned out enough to see. The back door was sliding glass, with vertical blinds that were only half closed. Not quite a block away, a streetlight burned, and they could see the silhouette of the two black-eyed kids.

Tap, tap, tap.

Dylan shouted, "Go away! We won't let you in!"

A voice from the other side of the door wailed eerily and then said, "*Pleeeeease, I'm just a little girl, and it's soooo cooooooold.*"

Noah whispered, "Is that door locked?"

Dylan's eyes went wide. He darted around the side of the refrigerator, ran to the door, and threw the lock. In the corner was a wooden broom handle his father had cut to fit in the track of the sliding glass door to help secure it. Dylan grabbed it and shoved it in place. Then he looked out the door. The two children stood as before.

"*Let uuuus in.*"

Dylan yelped when he felt Noah grip his arm and pull him away. "Let's lock your garage door, then all the entrances will be secure."

Dylan nodded. "And then we'll make sure all the first-floor windows are locked, too."

They rushed around the house, checking all the locks. Noah ran into a dining room chair and knocked it over with a crash. From upstairs, they heard a soft thump and a creak. They looked at each other, and Dylan put his finger to his lips. Noah nodded.

After they stood unmoving for a long time, Dylan took a deep breath and whispered, "Okay, now what?"

Noah thought a moment and said, "Information. We need to get more info on black-eyed kids."

"My laptop's over there," Dylan said, and they started for the living room. The power went out, and the lights died. "Really? Now? There goes the Wi-Fi."

Noah's voice broke like he was about to lose it. "Of course the power goes out."

Tap, tap, tap.

They whipped their heads around to the front door, though it wasn't visible in the dark.

Tap, tap, tap. "*Let ussss innnnn.*"

"Who's at the door?" a young voice asked.

Noah blurted out, "Dylan! It's your sister! She's downstairs!"

Noah yelled, "Wait, Ann Marie, don't!"

Tap, tap, tap.

In the dark, they heard the sound of the dead bolt lock unlatching and the click of the doorknob. Faint light filtered in through the door, barely illuminating Dylan's young sister. "Hello. Do you want to come in?"

"No!" Noah yelled when he saw the silhouettes of two children enter. Complete darkness returned when the door closed. He panicked, turned, and ran through the house to the kitchen. He unlocked the sliding glass door and tried opening it, but it wouldn't budge. He fought with it and then remembered the broom handle placed in the track for extra security. He pulled it out and flung it across the room. That was when Dylan's sister screamed. Noah slid open the door and ran into the night.

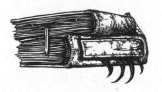

– CHAPTER 5 –

ZOFIA'S GOLEM

Down a city street that was almost narrow enough to be called an alley sat the Warszawski Teatr Ogrodowy, or Warsaw Garden Theater. *Warsaw* was part of its name because it was in the Polish city of Warsaw. The *Garden* part was a mystery because it sat on a street of buildings made of brick and stone, with no plants, trees, or flowers in sight. While some parts of the city in the spring of 1942 were in rubble and ruin due to air raids and artillery bombardment, the theater's street had been mostly spared. Still, frightening sounds were sometimes heard from nearby Krochmalna Street: the clank of turning treads on

German tanks, troop transports, the marching of the Dir-lewanger Brigade, shouts and orders, and, on occasion, gunfire.

The theater had existed for over sixty years. It had been popular before the Nazi invasion, with sold-out shows night after night. Now Warsaw's occupiers sought to destroy Polish culture by arresting and executing scholars and artists and closing schools, concert halls, newspapers, and theaters. But artists still painted and sculpted, underground concerts took place in undisclosed locations, and, though illegal, the Warsaw Garden Theater put on the ocassional secret theatrical performance with small casts and rarely more than a dozen people in attendance. Sometimes no one was in the audience, yet they would perform anyway because, as all actors know, the show must go on.

The first floor of the three-story redbrick edifice held the theater itself, a large stage, three hundred seats, and a lobby. The balcony was on the second floor, along with the dressing rooms for the actors. The costume room, prop room, business office, and a kitchen could be found on the third floor. Scenery was kept in the basement. There was also a sub-basement, a basement under the basement, and it was a secret. Other than storage, its sole purpose during the Third Reich's occupation of War-saw was to hide a Jewish girl named Zofia Blumen.

On a chilly March morning, an elderly man and woman walked up the sidewalk to the theater. Bypassing the main entrance, they turned down an alley and used a key to open a door that had a sign on it that said TYLKO AKTORZY, or ACTORS ONLY. The man and woman owned the theater; they were brother and sister. She walked with an erect posture and wore a green dress that covered her knees, a matching button-down blouse, and a green sweater over that. A small-brimmed black hat was on her head. The man was more relaxed in his gait and wore a brown suit, including a vest. As they walked indoors, he removed his hat, a brown fedora, and threw it spinning through the air, where it landed on a coatrack ten feet away. The man handed his sister a box, and they stepped onto a narrow staircase and separated; she went up, and he went down.

The basement had several light bulbs hanging from the ceiling with pull switches. He turned on two and then made his way to a scenery piece that looked like a large fireplace. An andiron in the fireplace held three logs. Though it looked heavy, the andiron and the logs were made of paper-mache and glued together into one piece. He lifted it up and placed it next to the fireplace. The andiron covered a trapdoor in the floor. Attached to the trapdoor was a wooden ladder leading down.

The man leaned over the trapdoor and called, "Zofia! Come up, sweetheart."

After several seconds, someone carrying a lantern walked beneath the trapdoor. A small girl with dark hair and pale skin looked up.

"Good morning, Uncle Wiktor." The girl lifted the lantern glass, blew out the candle, put the lantern down, and scrambled up the ladder.

Wiktor looked the girl over as she emerged from the fireplace. "I take it you've been sailing the high seas?"

Zofia held out her arms and spun, showing the costume she wore, including black boots and a ragged pair of canvas pants, held up with a wide leather belt. Her shirt was a black sleeveless pullover with red horizontal stripes. She removed the tricorn hat and bowed. When she put it back on, she placed her left hand on the hilt of the small sword attached to the belt. She wore an eye patch, but it had been turned up so both of her large brown eyes were visible.

"I'm Zofia the Lionhearted. Scourge of the seven seas!"

she said, and giggled, then scrunched her face in thought. "What's a scourge, Uncle Wiktor?"

He laughed and said, "You, Zofia, are a scourge to my patience."

Zofia pulled a rolled-up sheet of paper from her pocket and handed it to him. "I made you a picture, Uncle Wiktor. It's you and me, and we're playing hide-and-seek."

Wiktor unrolled the paper and studied it. "I see me. But I don't see you."

"That's because I'm hiding."

Wiktor laughed, which made Zofia beam. She loved his laugh, which was full and hearty and seemed to come from the very center of his being.

"When I go home, I will put this picture on my wall. Now come, my pirate queen; let's go up and have breakfast."

"Aye-aye," Zofia said.

On the way to the kitchen on the third floor, they stopped at the costume room. "A good actor never eats in their costume," Wiktor said.

Zofia rolled her eyes. "I know, Uncle Wiktor." She picked up a simple brown dress and slip-on shoes and disappeared into a dressing room.

Five minutes later she sat at the kitchen table next to Uncle Wiktor.

The box he'd carried in was on the table, and he passed it to Zofia. "I talked to Mr. Kucharski this morning. He was selling from his wheelbarrow things he's found. He discovered it in the rubble of the Luksusowy Apartments."

Zofia's eyes lit up, and she opened the box. She started to reach in, stopped, and looked up at Uncle Wiktor.

"Don't you like the doll, Zofia?"

She glanced down at it again and made a face. Though it looked nearly new, except for the broken cheek, she slowly shook her head.

"That's fine, my little angel. If you don't like it, you don't have to play with it." He put the box top back on. "I'll take it to the prop room."

His sister set down three plates of potato pancakes and sat across from Zofia.

"Thank you, Mrs. Danek." Zofia cut a piece of pancake with the side of a fork and pushed it into her mouth.

"You are welcome, my dear." Mrs. Danek spoke in a formal tone, each word properly enunciated.

As Zofia chewed, she looked at Mrs. Danek and then

to Wiktor and back again. "If you're Uncle Wiktor's sister, why don't I call you Auntie?"

Mrs. Danek smiled. "Because I'm not your aunt."

Wiktor gave Zofia a sad smile. "And I'm not really your uncle. You know that."

Having just placed a big piece of pancake in her mouth, Zofia nodded.

"Wiktor and I are very different people," Mrs. Danek said. "Wiktor is like a big, huggable rag doll, so it's right that you call him Uncle Wiktor."

Zofia laughed.

Wiktor put a hand to his mouth as if imparting a secret to Zofia. "While my sister is what you might call *aloof*."

"Wiktor!" Mrs. Danek said in protest.

"*Reserved, detached, snobbish.*" He leaned toward his sister with a mischievous smile. "And because she was once a famous actress, *diva*."

"Wiktor," Mrs. Danek repeated in a warning tone, but she smiled. Turning to Zofia, she said, "I behave like a proper Polish lady." Her expression softened. "Your mother and father were patrons of our theater. And though I may seem unaffectionate compared with my lovable brother, please know that I am happy you are here, that you are safe."

At the mention of her parents, Zofia put her fork on the table and gazed down. "I miss my matka and tatuś."

Wiktor and his sister exchanged a glance. He put his arm over the little girl's shoulders and pulled her close. "Of course you do."

"They were good people," Mrs. Danek said.

"Just like you," Wiktor said. "Which is why we must keep you safe, so the same thing doesn't happen to you."

"And that's why you have rules to follow," Mrs. Danek said. "What are those rules?"

Sniffing, Zofia looked up. "If anyone knocks on the doors, I must hurry down and hide in my room until you tell me it's safe."

"Yes," Mrs. Danek said.

"I am free to wander the theater when you are between shows, like now, but at night I must be careful not to turn on any lights or have my lantern seen in the windows."

"Very good," Wiktor said.

"When there are rehearsals or shows, I must hide in my room."

Mrs. Danek nodded. "The actors in our plays are good people, but you never know if someone might slip and say something to someone who is not so nice. And the next thing you know, the Schutzstaffel will force their way in and try to find you." Mrs. Danek made a face at the mention of the dreaded SS, the Nazi paramilitary force. "They are devils who take our Jewish friends and make them disappear. Even little angels like you."

Zofia licked her lips and nodded solemnly. "And I must never, ever leave the theater." Zofia pondered that and smiled. "It's a good thing I love the theater."

Wiktor put his big hand over her small one. "Are you ever scared when you're here alone at night?"

Zofia shook her head and pointed at the little kitchen window. "The scary stuff is out there."

Wiktor patted her hand.

"I almost got scared last night when I saw the giant gingerbread man on the other side of my room."

"Gingerbread man?" Mrs. Danek asked.

"Mmmm-hmmmm."

Mrs. Danek looked at her brother. "I don't know of any giant gingerbread man, do you?"

Wiktor thought. "No. Maybe it's a costume, but then it'd be in the costume room."

"It's not," Zofia said.

"In the sub-basement?" Wiktor asked.

Zofia nodded and took a bite of her pancake.

"Well then, you'll have to show me."

After breakfast, Zofia and Wiktor stopped briefly at the costume room so Zofia could put on a frilly pink dress and matching bonnet. "I'm Little Miss Muffet."

"Obviously."

They descended the staircase all the way to the basement; Wiktor once again moved the andiron and logs from the fireplace scenery, and he followed Zofia down the ladder into the sub-basement. Zofia's parents had been taken by the Schutzstaffel and put on a train to the concentration camp Treblinka. When that happened, Wiktor had taken his tools and walled off the stairs that led to the sub-basement. He then cut the trapdoor through the basement floor and moved the fireplace scenery over that and fashioned the secret andiron and logs doorway. The last thing he made was a room for Zofia. It was a small bedroom that Wiktor wired for electricity. He had painted the walls pink and given her a bed with a soft mattress. He'd put up an actor's mirror ringed with light bulbs over a small dressing table. It was also on that table that Zofia used her kredki, or crayons, to draw pictures, which she often gave to Wiktor.

Wiktor had added wiring for a light fixture in the ceiling, and into it, he put a red light bulb. Zofia thought the bulb was scary, because if the red light ever flashed, it meant that either Wiktor or Mrs. Danek had pressed a hidden button upstairs, and it was a signal that it was not safe for Zofia. She was to turn out all the lights in her room, hide, and not make a sound.

Only Zofia's room was wired for electricity in the sub-basement, so Wiktor lit the lantern that Zofia had left at the bottom of the ladder.

"Where is this giant gingerbread man you found?"

Zofia took the lantern from his hand and led him past the door to her room, to the far side of the sub-basement.

"Aha, this is where the oldest sets and scenery are stored," Wiktor said.

Zofia took his hand and guided him past rows of flats painted to look like buildings and forests, and one a castle. They turned right and passed a painted desert scene, and Zofia stopped before a flat painted to look like the deck of a sailing ship.

She pointed into the darkness. "There."

Wiktor took the lantern and stepped toward an alcove in the brick wall. The recess was eight feet high and five feet wide. He raised the lantern, gasped, and jumped back.

"See. It scared you, too," Zofia said, giggling.

They both approached the giant figure. It looked like

a man a child might sculpt from clay, but it was huge. It almost brushed the top of the eight-foot recess with its head. Its shoulders were so wide they touched each side of the five-foot-wide niche. Its features were minimal: round eyes and a round opening for a mouth. There wasn't a neck to speak of; the figure had a bullet-shaped head that sat directly on its shoulders. At the end of its long arms were large, simple hands. Each had a blocky thumb, but there were no individual fingers. Thick legs ended in big, squarish feet.

"Ohhhh," Wiktor said. "It is not a gingerbread man; it is a golem."

"What is a golem?" Zofia asked.

"Wait a moment." Wiktor went to fetch a couple of small tables from among the set pieces and found a candelabra as well. He put the tables near the golem and put Zofia's lantern on one and the candelabra on the other. He lit the four candles in it, and with the lantern, it provided enough light to see the golem well.

"I didn't make the connection when you said a giant gingerbread man. About fifteen years ago we produced a play called *Der Goylem*, which is Yiddish for *The Golem*. If we produced it today, the Nazis would storm the theater and arrest us all."

"Why?"

"It was written by a Jewish playwright about a rabbi in Prague who made a golem to defend the Jews and destroy their enemies."

"Is it a real golem?" Zofia asked.

Wiktor chuckled and rubbed her head. "Golems aren't real, sweetheart; it's only a folktale."

"Oh." Zofia sounded disappointed and then said, "Tell me more about the play."

Wiktor took a moment to collect his thoughts. "Well, in the play, the rabbi makes a golem from clay, and the actor who played the rabbi was also a real sculptor, and he would, during each performance, actually work on it, adding a piece during one show, another piece during the next show, and so on. By the time the play's run ended, he had completed this giant golem. If my memory serves me right, it took three hundred pounds of clay."

"Wow."

Wiktor stepped forward and ran his hand over the golem. "In the play, once the rabbi brought the golem to life, we had an actor in a costume that resembled this giant rendering."

Zofia put a hand on the golem. "How did he bring the golem to life?"

Wiktor looked around, spied a chair, pulled it over, and sat. "It's been a long time; let me see if I can remember. In the play, the rabbi put a shem in the golem's mouth, which brought it to life."

"What's a shem?"

"It's one of the Hebrew names for God, written on a piece of paper. Wait." Wiktor wagged his index finger as he remembered something else. "There was also another way to bring a golem to life. You had to use Hebrew symbols to write the word *truth* on the golem's forehead."

"*Truth?*"

Wiktor nodded. "And when the golem finished its work, whoever created it could erase the last letter, and that changed it to the word *dead*, or *death*, and the golem would break into pieces." Wiktor paused as he pointed to his left and then to his right. "Hebrew is read from right to left, so it would really be the first letter you would erase." Wiktor rubbed his chin. "Fascinating folklore."

"I wish it was real." Zofia laid her cheek against the clay monstrosity. "A golem would make me feel safer when I get scared."

Wiktor leaped from his seat. "Well, if it will make you feel better, let's see if we can find out how to spell *truth* with Hebrew letters. Whenever you're scared, you can write it on the golem and pretend it awakens to protect you."

Wiktor and Zofia rushed upstairs to the third-floor prop room. Wiktor explained, "So many plays have scenes that take place in libraries, so I began collecting old books." They passed shelves that held all kinds of glassware, headed down an aisle that had all manner of stage props, and stopped at more shelves that were crammed full of books. Wiktor ran his finger along the spines and titles of each work. "One of these books was a Hebrew dictionary with a Polish translation. I hope it's still here. Ah! Yes. Here it is."

Zofia and Wiktor spent the next hour in the kitchen working on how to spell *truth* in Hebrew. Once Zofia could make a good copy of it, Wiktor then made her write it backward.

"Remember, Hebrew is written right to left. So it seems that if you want it to work, it should be written that way, yes?"

"I guess." Zofia didn't sound convinced, but after several tries, Zofia could write *truth* in Hebrew.

תמא

"Very good, Zofia. But now I have theater business to attend to, so I need to work."

"Can we play hide-and-seek this afternoon?"

Wiktor smiled. "Of course. And after supper, before Mrs. Danek and I leave for the night, I'll read you another chapter from your book."

The next morning Zofia was in the costume room looking for something fun to wear when she heard the *actors only* door slam shut downstairs. She ran to the balustrade and looked down, fighting the urge to call out to Uncle Wiktor. Though it wasn't one of the official rules, she knew to be quiet until she was sure it was either him or Mrs. Danek. Someone was coming up the stairs, and then she saw it was Mrs. Danek.

"Good morning, Mrs. Danek. I'll go tell Uncle Wiktor I'm already up here."

It was then that Zofia noticed Mrs. Danek had been crying.

"No, child. Wiktor is not with me."

"Where is he?"

"Let's go to the kitchen." She gave Zofia a strained smile. "And I will make you a hot chocolate."

Zofia followed Mrs. Danek into the kitchen, her stomach beginning to twist in worry. She sat at the table, too scared to say anything.

Mrs. Danek kept a stoic expression as she went about making their drinks until she finally set a steaming cup in front of Zofia. Mrs. Danek sat with her coffee cup and saucer. After taking a sip, Mrs. Danek put her cup down, and Zofia saw that she was trembling.

"We must be strong."

"Ma'am?"

"Something happened last night, Zofia." Mrs. Danek pulled a handkerchief from a sleeve and dabbed at her eyes. "The SS came to our house and took away my brother."

"Uncle Wiktor," Zofia said in a small voice. "Why? He's not Jewish."

"They said he is a homosexual."

"What's that?" Zofia asked.

Mrs. Danek brought her fist down on the table, making Zofia jump. She spoke with an angry expression. "Another excuse the Nazis use to kill people who are not like them." Mrs. Danek took Zofia's hand and squeezed too hard. "When will it end, Zofia?" Mrs. Danek's expression twisted with grief. "When will they leave us alone?"

Zofia stared at Mrs. Danek through tears.

"I'm sorry, Zofia, this is not a topic for children, but we live in terrible times. You need to know so you'll understand why it is so important you hide." Mrs. Danek sat up straight and cleared her throat. "Last night the Schutzstaffel rounded up dozens of men, women, and children. Jews, gypsies, and, as they accused your uncle, homosexuals. They took them in trucks to the Palmiry Forest. They were forced out of the trucks and made to stand in a line...and...and..." Unable to say more, Mrs. Danek put her face in her hands and sobbed.

They both cried, and though Mrs. Danek was not an affectionate person, she held Zofia until their hot drinks turned cold in their cups. Eventually Mrs. Danek got up and drifted out of the kitchen. Zofia left her cup untouched, went to her room in the sub-basement, turned off the light, and fell onto her bed. She thought of Uncle Wiktor and cried.

Zofia lay on her bed a long time; it was probably afternoon, but in the sub-basement, it was always night. At first, she had the frightening thought that the theater was on fire, and then she realized that the red emergency light on her ceiling was flashing. Someone was in the theater, and it was someone Mrs. Danek wanted her to hide from.

Zofia left her room, and though the darkness was complete, she knew the way to the ladder that led up to the trapdoor. She stood there and listened as her heart fluttered like the wings of a small bird. She could hear heavy footsteps overhead. After several minutes, the footsteps got louder, and she heard voices.

Mrs. Danek sounded panicked. "Please, there's no one down here. It's simply a basement, storage for the theater."

A man's harsh voice barked, "Search everywhere." It made Zofia jump.

After long minutes, a terrible thing happened. From above she saw a square of light as the hiding place of the trapdoor was discovered. She retreated far enough so that she wouldn't be seen by anyone looking down.

"Oberführer! Over here. I have found something." Another male voice.

The harsh voice returned. "Interesting. And what will we find down here, I wonder."

Mrs. Danek cried now. "There's nothing down there, just more storage."

"Sturmann," the harsh voice barked.

"Yes, Oberführer?"

"Search below."

"Yes, Oberführer."

Mrs. Danek was pleading, "No, no, no."

The trapdoor darkened as a man passed through and descended. Zofia backed up more and saw another German soldier follow the first down. She turned and ran to her room. Inside, she rushed to her dressing table and felt around, grabbing a crayon. Because of the dark, she wasn't sure which color. On her bedside table, she reached for matches and her lantern, nearly knocking it over. At the door of her room, she peeked out as the two soldiers held up small metal boxes the size of a deck of playing cards. They each flipped a switch, and she saw they were flashlights. When both beams of light were aimed in another direction, Zofia swept from her room and went the other way, using a hand to feel along the scenery. She stopped when she thought she was far enough from them, and with shaking hands used a match to light the lantern's candle.

"Oberführer!" one of the soldiers called out. "You'll want to see this. A room with toys and children's clothes."

From above, the oberführer addressed Mrs. Danek. "A Jewish child, no doubt. Do you know the penalty for harboring Jews?"

Mrs. Danek cried out, "Please. Please don't hurt her."

A minute later Zofia heard the oberführer, now in the sub-basement, at her room. "She's not far. Find her."

Zofia rushed through the scenery, by the painted flats and set pieces, and looked up at the golem. She pulled one of the tables that Uncle Wiktor had put there earlier directly in front of the golem. She stood on it, but it was not high enough. As she heard the soldiers coming closer, she put the other table on top of the first and climbed up. She would have to stand on tiptoes and reach high, but she could do it. She envisioned the Hebrew spelling of *truth*. She squinted in concentration and began to write the word in green crayon from right to left on the golem's forehead.

Light swept over her and then returned.

"Here, Oberführer. She is here."

Zofia didn't turn but took the time to finish the word. When she was done, she climbed carefully from the tables, turned, and walked toward the soldier. Another joined him. Both carried rifles over their shoulders.

The oberführer approached with an arrogant stride. To Zofia, he looked like a monster. His hat was gray with a black visor. On the front was a silver eagle with its wings spread. It stood on a wreath encircling a swastika. Below that was a silver skull and crossbones. The collar of his gray wool jacket was black with some kind of insignia on it. A shiny black leather belt encircled high on his waist and held a pistol in a covered holster. He wore jodhpurs, pants that were tight from the knees to the ankles, but puffy along the thighs, and they were tucked into black boots.

The oberführer stared down at Zofia through round, rimless glasses. "You are Jewish, yes?"

Zofia didn't speak.

The oberführer knelt down in front of Zofia. "Do you know how I knew you were here?" When she didn't answer, he continued. "Last night, when we arrested the deviant you know as Wiktor, his bedroom had pictures on his wall. Pictures drawn by a child. Many of the pictures, I think, were of Wiktor and you. Am I right?"

Zofia glared at the officer, her hands in tight fists at her sides.

"So, I am thinking, there is no little girl living in the house he shares with his sister. If he spends all his time at either home or at his theater, where does he know this girl? And this afternoon, as I am walking by the theater with two of my soldiers, it suddenly comes to me. He is hiding the little girl. Why would a man hide a girl? Because she is a Jewish girl. And since we searched his home last night, where would he hide her?" The oberführer swept out his hands dramatically. "Here, in the theater, of course."

The SS officer stood and put his hands behind his back and stood ramrod straight. "You will come with us."

Continuing to glare, Zofia spoke, "No."

The oberführer took a step so that he towered over Zofia. "Do you know who I am?"

Zofia shook her head.

His voice dropped to a low tone that was almost a growl. "I am SS-Sturmbrigade Dirlewanger Oberführer Otto Kraus of the Thirty-Sixth Waffen Grenadier Division."

There was a moment of quiet, and in a small voice, Zofia asked, "Do you know who I am?"

The SS officer raised his eyebrows. "Who?"

"I am Zofia, a Jewish girl." Her eyes remained fierce, but a smile broke on her face. "And I have a golem."

From behind her, she heard the golem knocking the small tables from its path, and then the low, grating sound of its shoulders rubbing the wall as it emerged from its alcove. The weighty footsteps of the clay giant echoed in the sub-basement. As the soldiers' attention was locked on the eight-foot-tall clay man emerging from darkness, Zofia rushed between a soldier and the oberführer and turned as the golem took another step and lifted its hands. Its eyes glowed white, as did the Hebrew spelling of *truth* on its forehead.

The oberführer reached for his pistol, and the two soldiers took the rifles from their shoulders. Zofia ran, and gunfire barked before she took ten steps. By the time she reached her room, the men were screaming. By the time she reached the ladder, they made no noise at all.

Zofia climbed quickly and found Mrs. Danek crying as she knelt by the trapdoor.

She gasped when she saw Zofia and pulled her into her arms. They held each other a long time.

CHAPTER 6

THE DOOR IN THE WOODS

Mady found the door in the woods on a Saturday morning. Normally Mady spent Saturdays in the company of her bestie, Anya, but they'd been arguing. The argument started at school when Mady kept talking about her favorite band and Anya said they weren't that good. Later Anya said she wanted to see a new superhero movie, and Mady got revenge by saying the trailer looked terrible. It went back and forth like that, getting worse and worse. Finally, Anya said something about how cute Marcus Shepherd was, and Mady made a gagging sound. That's when the fireworks really started. They argued, they called each other names, and they said something that neither meant, that they didn't want to be friends anymore.

So Mady hiked through the woods alone, in cutoffs and a tank top and with her dark hair pulled into a ponytail. After hiking for almost an hour, she strolled near a small meadow surrounded by trees. She was going to pass it by, but she saw an old doll lying in the dirt and half covered with pine needles. She went to pick it up, but a centipede popped out of the hole of its missing left eye.

"Ewwww."

She watched it crawl along the doll's face and then looked up to see an ancient door in the middle of the meadow. It stood, anchored to the ground, with nothing attached to it on any side. A door all by itself. The wood was scarred, and the natural grain wove designs across its surface, which in places looked like faces and figures. The hinges and knob were tarnished brass. A darker wood formed the frame. It was a small door, only as tall as her hip, and half that wide. High grass filled the clearing and was circled by cypress, ash, and oak trees.

Mady sat in the warm grass and studied it. She leaned forward, put her hand on the doorknob, and tried to twist it, but it was locked. And then she wondered how to un-lock it, because there was no keyhole.

She regretted her argument with Anya now. When someone found something as bizarre as this, they should share it with somebody. She sighed, then smiled. She would tell Anya. It would speed up their reconciliation.

Mady started back through the clearing in the direc-tion of their neighborhood. As she got to the ring of big trees, she stopped and cocked her head. Someone whis-tled a melody in the distance. She crouched behind an ash tree and waited. When it sounded as if the person was in the clearing, she peered around the tree trunk. The tall grass stirred as something moved through it. If it wasn't for the whistling, she'd have probably thought it was a squirrel or a fox or a raccoon. She saw the whistler and gasped. Like the door, he was tiny. His head just stuck out above the grass. His flesh was blue, and his large eyes were dark brown. He was bald, and his ears were pointed at the tops. Every now and then she could just see enough of his shoulders to know he was shirtless, though he wore red suspenders. The little man stopped in front of the door, reached up with a tiny arm, and knocked three times. He grasped the doorknob and turned it, and the door opened. The small person crossed the threshold and closed the door. The figure should have crossed over the doorjamb and exited out the other side, but the little person was gone, as if the door actually led somewhere else.

Mady stared for a full minute and then ran for Anya's house.

When Anya opened the door, Mady smiled sheepishly and said, "Hi."

Anya gave her an icy stare. But she thawed when Mady apologized and admitted that, yes, Marcus Shepherd was pretty darn cute. Forty-five minutes later they were hiking through the woods, back in the direction of the small door.

"So a short man went through the door?" Anya asked.

"Not short. Small. He was about this high." Mady held her hand flat at midthigh.

"No way."

"And he was blue and had pointy ears."

"Like a fairy?"

Mady nodded. "Or an elf."

After a while, Anya asked, "How much farther?"

"Right past those trees."

Anya grinned at Mady and then took off running. Mady

caught up with her just past the ring of trees, where Anya stood with eyes wide and mouth open.

"What's the matter?" Mady asked.

Anya pointed into the middle of the clearing. "It's a little door in the woods."

"That's what I said."

Anya looked at her with an amazed expression. "I thought you were playing. I thought we were going to make up a story about a fairy door, or something—wait a minute. Did you really see a fairy or elf go through the door?"

"Yes."

Cautiously, they approached the door, and something hit Mady in the back of the head.

"Ow!"

Another pine cone flew through the air and hit Anya. "Ouch!"

There was rustling in the brush, and a figure came out.

"It's your brother," Anya said.

"Devin! That hurt." Mady rubbed her head.

"Sorry."

"Not to mention that you scared us," Anya said.

"Doubly sorry."

A few years older than them, Devin was tall with brown hair in loose curls. He had a deep brown tan because he liked doing things outdoors: fishing, canoeing, rock climbing, and hiking. Judging by the hiking boots he wore, that was what he was currently engaged in. He took his pack from his back, retrieved a bottle of water, and tossed it to Mady. She took a drink and passed it to Anya.

He took out another bottle, opened it, and started to take a drink, but he stopped long enough to ask, "Do Mom and Dad know you're out here?"

"Don't tell."

He looked at her a moment, took a drink, and said, "You're not supposed to go this far out in the woods." She looked at him, her eyes all sorrowful, like she was close to crying. "Okay, I won't tell," Devin said.

Mady's face instantly brightened. "Thanks."

"So what are you doing out here?"

The girls looked at each other.

"Come on, I said I wouldn't tell on you."

Anya, eyes still on Mady, shrugged.

"Okay," Mady said. "I was showing something to Anya."

Devin started to respond but looked past Mady.

At first, his brows furrowed, and then they raised up. "What's that?"

"That's what I was showing Anya."

"It's a door," Anya said.

"I found it earlier today."

Devin pushed past them. "How weird. I mean, it's just a door—"

"A tiny door," Mady added.

"But sticking up in the woods with nothing around it." He rubbed a hand over the top of the doorframe. Devin looked at one side of the door and then took a step to examine the other. He grabbed the doorknob one-handed and attempted to turn it. All it earned him was a grunt. He grabbed each side of the doorframe and, grunting and groaning, attempted to lift it. His grip slipped, and he fell.

Mady and Anya sat next to him and scrutinized the door.

"So the little man you saw opened the door and went through?" Anya said.

"Yes."

"What little man?" Devin asked.

Mady told him what she'd seen.

"Now you're just making stuff up."

"No, I'm not."

Anya leaned forward and tried to turn the doorknob. "It's locked now."

"I know. It was before," Mady said.

"How did the little man open it?" Anya asked.

Mady pointed at the door. "He knocked three times, turned the doorknob, and went through."

Devin leaned forward, knocked three times, and turned the knob. It opened with a click. They all exchanged a glance and got on their hands and knees. Mady timidly pulled the door all the way open.

"Whoa," Devin muttered.

Through the doorframe they saw a great big meadow of the greenest grass. In the distance was a lake the color of a blue jewel.

"I'm going to check it out." Devin started through the door, barely fitting.

"Wait, Devin," Mady said, but he was already through.

He stood up on the other side, and they could see only the backs of his legs, from the knees down. Mady looked at her friend a second and then followed her brother through. Anya went last.

They stood next to one another, gazing at the land-scape before them.

"You swear you saw a little blue man?" Devin asked.

"Cross my heart."

"I think I believe you, because it's like a—a—a—"

"Fairy tale," Mady whispered.

"Yeah."

High in the sky over the lake, the sun shone with a soft yellow glow that allowed them to look directly at it without hurting their eyes. Under the sun, a rainbow stretched from horizon to horizon, the colors incredibly deep. The air was full of brightly hued butterflies the size of their hands. Wildflowers grew all about the meadow in every imaginable shape and color. Bees darted from flower to flower, and instead of buzzing, they hummed a melody.

"Let's go check out the lake," Devin said, and started walking.

"He's hoping to discover a new fishing spot," Mady told Anya.

They laughed and followed after Devin, going down a hill and toward a small stream of clear water.

Devin knelt, cupped his hands, and drank some by the time his sister and Anya caught up. "Wow. It's really good."

Mady and Anya knelt and drank. Water erupted,

splashing Mady. She wiped her eyes and looked at the creek. A school of small fish was just under the surface. When they looked closer, they saw they weren't exactly fish.

"Look," Mady said in awe. "Mermaids."

Little mermaids, not even six inches long, swam back and forth, smiling up at them. Mady reached down and put her index finger in the water. The mermaids swam around it, splashing along the surface.

Mady laughed. "It tickles."

Devin watched a moment, then fell back and sat. "This doesn't make any sense."

"No, but it's cool," Anya said.

Devin stood. "Let's explore."

"Bye, little mermaids," Mady said with a wave.

Their journey led to a tree line and into the woods. Birds of all shapes, colors, and sizes flew among the trees, singing beautiful songs. They followed a small path. At one point a bird so black as to reflect a blue sheen flew directly overhead, and its birdsong became words.

Mady is the brave one; she explored and found the door.

"It knows my name," Mady said.

Anya is the beauty that all the boys adore.

"Awww," she said.

And Devin is the explorer; he'll travel distant shores.

"Cool."

The bird then flew down right in front of them and hovered like a hummingbird.

While you're here in this land, there's something you should mind,

If you go searching 'round, be careful what you find.

The bird flitted up to the right, then to the left, and flew off into the trees.

Mady stared after the bird. "Was that a warning? A threat?"

"Maybe we should go back," Anya said.

"Ah, it was just a bird. Let's look around some more," Devin said. "If things get any stranger, we'll leave."

They came out of the woods into a meadow even more lush than the last one. In the distance, a large, four-legged animal was facing away from them.

"A horse," Mady said.

"A big horse," Devin said. "Big as a Clydesdale."

Crossing the meadow, they stopped ten yards from it. Anya made kissy noises, trying to get its attention. The animal extended its great neck, saw them, and fully turned.

Mady gasped. "It's a unicorn."

They stared at the mythical beast as it scrutinized them.

Anya suggested, "Let's get closer."

Before they moved forward, the unicorn started to breathe hard, its flanks expanding with each breath. Its nut-brown eyes went bloodred. The unicorn snorted, and smoke blew from its nostrils. It pawed at the ground and then lowered its head so that its horn pointed at them like a three-foot sword.

"Run!" Mady shouted.

A moment later the sound of the unicorn's hooves thundered. They raced for the tree line, the galloping beast closing the distance. The ground trembled as the unicorn grew nearer and nearer. They made it to the trees just as they felt the monster's breath on their necks, and charged into the woods. The hoof sounds stopped, but they kept running for several more minutes and then slowed to a walk.

"I thought we were goners," Mady said, breathing hard and looking behind.

"Almost." Anya was equally out of breath.

Looking overhead, Devin said, "It's getting dark. We better head home."

Retracing their steps, they exited the woods, crossed

the stream, and walked up the meadow. They got in sight of the little door and stopped.

"There are two doors now," Mady said.

Two little identical doors stood next to each other in the fairy-tale meadow.

"Did you notice two doors before?" Anya asked.

Devin thought a moment. "When we came through, I was so amazed I don't think I looked back at the door."

They approached the doors.

"We'll look in both to make sure we pick the right one," Devin said.

The ground started to shake with the sound of pounding hooves.

"The unicorn found us!" Mady yelled.

"Which door?" Anya screamed.

"I think it's this one," Devin said, knocking three times and pushing it open. Gesturing rapidly for the door, he yelled, "Go, go, go!"

Anya dove through and Mady followed. Devin dropped to his knees and went through just as the unicorn stuck its snout through the door, its teeth clicking as it bit empty air. When it removed its nose, Devin kicked the door closed.

They stood together in darkness.

"Is it nighttime?" Devin said.

"If it is, Dad's going to kill me," Anya said.

"You'll be in trouble, too," Devin said to Mady.

Mady started to point out that he'd be in trouble as well, but she noticed something and stamped her foot. Then she knelt down and ran her hands over the ground. "The floor, it's wood."

Devin got down on a knee and felt around. "You're right; it's a hardwood floor. We're not in the woods. I think we went through the wrong door."

Anya dropped to her knees. "What do we do now?"

They were quiet a few moments, then Devin said, "We go back through the door we just came through and then go through the other one."

"But we should wait a little bit. Give the unicorn time to leave," Mady said.

"Where do you think we are?" Anya asked.

"I don't know," Devin said. "Can't see a thing."

They were startled by a thump. Three seconds later it repeated, and again. Each time it got a little bit louder, becoming booms that shook the floor.

"Something's coming," Devin said, his voice wary. "Something big."

Mady jumped. "Let's find somewhere to hide."

They hurried away from the little door, hands held before them in the dark, and after a moment, Mady said, "A tree. We can hide behind it."

A second later they were blinded when a monstrously big door crashed opened and light flooded in. A creature entered carrying a very big lantern and closed the door. It was twenty feet tall at least. The lantern held a three-foot candle, throwing light and showing them they were in a cavernous room. They also learned they weren't cowering behind a tree but were huddled behind a table leg. The tabletop was seven feet up from the ground, twenty feet long, and ten feet wide. The giant strode to a fireplace big enough to park a school bus in. Long lengths of trees were piled in there, and the giant worked at starting a fire.

It had no hair on its head or anywhere else on its body. It was incredibly obese; great rolls of greasy fat hung around its neck, belly, and hips. The skin on its arms and legs wobbled when it moved. Nearly naked, it wore only a loincloth pieced together from animal hides.

Anya's voice was so high she nearly squeaked when she whispered, "What is that thing?"

"Shhh," Devin said, finger to his lips.

When the fire started to burn, the giant moved with

great strides across the room. At the table, it pulled out the gigantic chair. It sat, and all they could see of the giant was from its waist down.

From overhead came a crack and a sucking noise. A second later something fell from the tabletop to the floor in front of them. The cracking and slurping continued, and they tiptoed over to what had fallen. It looked like a white tree branch that had been broken nearly in two. Peering into the break, they saw that it was hollow.

Mady whispered, "It's a bone."

After another snap and slurp, Devin said, "The giant is cracking open bones and sucking out the marrow."

More cracked bones fell to the floor.

They took the time to look around the room, feeling it was safe enough to walk around as long as they kept under the table and out of the giant's sight. There were no windows, and the walls were made of great stones mortared together. The ceiling was the underside of a thatched roof about thirty feet above.

"There's the door we came in." Anya pointed next to the roaring fireplace, where there was a small door that looked exactly like the one they'd come through. Next to it was the colossal door through which the giant entered.

Mady pointed to the other side of the big door. "Or is that the one we came through?" There was an identical tiny door.

Anya felt sick as she pointed around the room. "Or is it any of the other ones?" Every wall in the room had one giant door with a tiny door on either side.

"Two small doors on each wall. That's eight possibilities," Devin said.

"Let's wait," Anya said. "If the giant leaves, we can peek in each door, see which gets us to the meadow."

"And go through, and then through the other one to our woods," Devin said.

They sat on the floor under the table and listened as the giant sucked from countless bones, the occasional one falling. The giant must've had quite an appetite, because it ate for a long time, but finally it burped long and low. Pushing back its chair, it stood with a tremendous groan, scratched at its backside, picked up its lantern, and walked through the huge door on the right side of the fireplace.

Mady, Anya, and Devin stepped out from underneath the table and by the light from the fireplace looked around the room.

"Let's check out the doors," Devin said. They started at the wall with the fireplace.

They knelt at a door, and Mady took a breath before knocking three times. Anya turned the knob and pulled it open. They peered through into a night sky. Not too far away were several people standing and dancing around a blazing bonfire. Sparks flew up, twisting and twirling in the night. People chanted as they moved in a circle around the fire.

"It's a bunch of old women." Anya felt chilled when she saw that some wore conical hats, and some were bent and haggard, with large hooked noses and warts on their faces. They held long skeletal fingers out to the flames, moving them in rhythm with their incantations. One old hag turned in their direction, her left eye three times the size of her right, and she pointed at them and hissed like a snake.

"Witches," Mady blurted out.

Devin slammed the little door. "You guys try that one." He pointed at another door. "I'll check those over there." He indicated the opposite wall and started for it. "Be careful."

Mady and Anya got to the next door and down on their knees.

Mady started to knock but stopped when Anya gasped. "Oh no."

Motion from the far corner caught their attention. An animal about the size of a calf scurried out of it in a zigzag pattern toward the table.

"Is that—" Anya started.

"An enormous rat." Mady gagged; there were things she thought were gross, and rats were near the top of that list, right under cockroaches.

Mady pulled Anya behind the giant-sized fireplace tools next to the raging fire. They peeked around the humongous poker, fireplace shovel, and whisk broom at the creature, which was covered in oily black fur. A five-foot bald tail trailed behind it like a dead appendage. Its black bulbous eyes were the size and shape of halved baseballs, and its nose twitched, making its long whiskers waggle as it tracked odors.

"Devin," Mady whispered.

He, too, had seen the rat and frozen, hoping it wouldn't notice him if he didn't move.

The rat stopped before the broken bones the giant had dropped. It sniffed at one and then lifted its snout high and sniffed some more. It bypassed the bones and started for Mady's brother.

Devin's eyes grew bigger the closer the rat got to him. Finally, it stopped before him, sniffed, and then hissed.

Devin punched it in the nose, to no effect. It opened its jaws, displaying yellow foot-long rodent incisors.

Devin turned and started running toward Mady and Anya, but the rat darted to cut him off. Devin ran for the nearest small door. He dropped to his knees without slowing and slid up to it, rapidly knocked, pulled it open, and crawled through. The rat got there a second later and poked its nose in. Its paws scrabbled on the floor, nails clicking, as it attempted to push its bulk through the door. Finally, it pulled its nose from the doorframe and returned to one of the bones under the table. It chewed on it a moment, then grasped it in its mouth and wandered off the way it had come in, pushing through a large crack in the opposite corner.

Mady and Anya ran from their hiding place to the open door.

"Devin, it's gone; come on out," Mady called.

There was no answer. They got on their knees to peek through the door.

"It's dark," Anya said.

"It's like outer space," Mady muttered.

Far off, dim lights floated and darted this way and that. Mady reached her hand through the door. "Brrrrr, it's super cold." She shouted, "Devin!"

A moment later he replied as though through an echoing canyon. "Mady?"

"This way, Devin!"

"Mady, helllllppppp!"

A second later Devin popped through the door so instantaneously that the girls screamed and jumped away. Halfway through the door, Devin grasped the jamb with one hand and reached for them with his other. Covered in a layer of frost, he shivered, and his eyes bugged out in fear.

"Help, q-q-q-q-quick, before it g-g-g-g-gets me." His teeth chattered from the cold.

Mady took one of his hands, and Anya took the other. At the same instant, one of the lights floated up behind Devin. It was as big as a house and hung from the end of a long, organic tendril that trailed off into the blackness. They pulled Devin into the room, and he knelt there catching his breath. A pale snakelike appendage pushed through the little door and whipped around Devin's legs.

"Don't let it get me!" he screamed.

The tentacle yanked Devin back through the door, but he managed to grab the jamb. Mady rushed forward and grabbed her brother's right wrist; Anya got him by his left.

"Pull!" Mady screamed.

They backed up a step and then another. The thing that had Devin started pulling harder. Mady and Anya doubled their efforts and gained a little more ground. It was like a game of tug-of-war, and Devin was the rope.

A second tentacle crossed the threshold; it reached past the first and wrapped around Devin's chest. It tightened, and Devin groaned as it squeezed.

Another step and they had managed to drag Devin farther back. Mady thought that if one of them could close the door on the tentacles, they might let go of her brother. But to close the door, Mady or Anya would have to release Devin, and neither girl was strong enough to hold him alone.

"Keep going," Mady growled.

Anya grunted as she pulled.

Then the tentacles relaxed their grip. With no resistance, the girls stumbled several feet. Devin sucked in air as the tentacle around his chest loosened.

When they came to a stop, Anya said, "Keep pulling until they let him go."

They made it easily back another step, and another. Mady and Anya smiled at each other, and then the tentacles went taut and tugged with incredible strength. All three kids were yanked into the air. Devin passed through the door. Anya smacked into the wall on the right side of the door, and Mady struck the left.

Anya was the first to wake up, moaning as she touched the bump on her head. The room was freezing because the little door was still open. She managed to close it by kicking at it, and then she crawled to Mady. She lay there with closed eyes and a bruise starting to show on her forehead. Anya shook her and whispered her name until she woke.

Mady blinked a few times and then sat bolt upright. "Where's Devin?"

Anya looked down and shook her head.

Mady knocked on the door and opened it, peering into the darkness. "I can't leave him."

"Don't get so close. One of those things might get you."

Mady scooted all the way to the opposite wall and sat cross-legged. "I have to wait for him."

Anya thought to argue, but instead she sat next to her friend and hugged her. After several minutes, Anya stood and looked into the other doors until she found the one that opened onto the green meadow.

She poked her head past the doorframe and made sure the unicorn was gone. The floor shook, indicating the return of the giant. Anya took her friend's hand, pulled her to her feet, and led her to the little door, and eventually home.

– CHAPTER 7 –

FROM THE DEPTHS OF DARK LAKE

At first, Simon Kolchak thought Lucas was just messing around. Later on, he thought he had mental issues. And now? What he thinks now takes a lot of explanation.

Simon met Lucas King on the first day of the past school year. Before that, he'd been in another district. Lucas's parents flip houses for a living, meaning they buy old, run-down homes, fix them up, and sell them for a profit. Lucas changed school districts because his parents were doing their biggest flip to date. They'd bought Lakewood House, out past Carrol Road and on the shore of Dark Lake. It was going to be a long restoration, so the family moved into the house.

The last resident had been a scientist who taught physics at the university. He bought the place in the 1970s. Something happened, and he was fired from the university in the late 1990s. He secluded himself at Lakewood House, which sits on twenty-eight acres, and started doing experiments on his own. A dozen years later, he disappeared and was never seen again. Simon thought it was pretty cool that an honest-to-goodness mad scientist used to live in his neighborhood.

Simon's family lived on Carrol Road, about a mile from Lakewood House, and he and Lucas started hanging out together.

The first time Simon went over, Lucas gave him a tour of the property. At one point they stood on the dock that extended out into the lake. It was long enough to tie off several boats. Dark Lake was well named. Because of the dark sediment that made up the lake bed, the lake water was dark, and at night and on cloudy days, it was black. Behind them was the house, which had been modern architecture in the 1960s. It was dated now, and obvious that no one had cared for it for years. The flat-roofed house had three stories, and the back of the house faced the lake and had a half-circle deck on each story. A portion of the second-floor deck had collapsed.

French doors opened onto the decks from each bedroom as well as the living room downstairs.

The boys went to the back of the house. Lucas's parents had already started renovating and torn down a couple of non-load-bearing walls, dumping the debris in a pile by the ground-floor deck. The only thing that wasn't broken drywall and wood was an ancient doll with a cracked porcelain face.

"Wanna see something really cool?" Lucas asked.

Simon nodded, and Lucas led him down an overgrown path through the woods. After a five-minute hike, they emerged into a clearing that held a huge barn.

"The people who built the house had horses and used it as stables."

Simon gave a *hmmmph* to show that he didn't think it was as cool as Lucas had suggested.

Lucas gave him a grin and said, "But that's not what Dr. Canfield used it for."

"You mean the mad scientist?"

"Yeah. Dr. Howard Canfield. He used it as his laboratory. Come see."

The main door was padlocked, but Lucas had a key. He slid open the door, and they stepped in. Dr. Canfield had removed all the stalls, the hayloft, and everything else that made it a barn and turned it into one big laboratory. Lucas pushed up a large switch by the door, and bright overhead lights blinked on.

"Dad thinks that in the years since Canfield vanished, some kids got in and vandalized the place." A lot of the lab tables had been overturned, and broken Pyrex laboratory glassware was scattered around the floor. The back half of the barn looked as if someone had tried to start a fire. Scorch marks reached up that wall to the ceiling as well as along the floor.

They spent more time in the lab, wandering around, picking up interesting things, and going through Dr. Canfield's desk drawers. Simon got to one corner of the barn that was in dark shadows. It was by the scorch-marked wall, where the overhead lights were broken and dangling. A huge piece of canvas covered something that was ten feet wide and fifteen feet tall.

He pulled down the canvas. "Check this out."

"Whoa," Lucas said.

It was a big machine. The face of it was covered with dials and gauges, knobs and buttons. What looked like three small go-cart steering wheels were lined up in a row, and next to them was an oversized switch, the kind you have to push all the way up to engage. Different sizes of pipes ran in and out of the machine.

Through autumn, winter, and the first of spring, Simon spent more time with Lucas. Every now and then they'd go into the barn and mess around in the lab. Things changed when Lucas called Simon one day in May and had him come over. Simon found him in the barn, and Lucas immediately called him over to Canfield's desk and pulled open a drawer. "I found a false bottom in here. When I took it out, I discovered this." He pulled out a large leather-bound journal.

Because they'd just been studying Stanley and Livingstone in history class, Simon paraphrased that famous quote, "Dr. Canfield's, I presume?"

Lucas laughed, opened it up, and riffled the pages. It was handwritten in hastily scrawled cursive. There were formulas included, as well as diagrams of lab machines. "It's hard to read. Canfield's handwriting is terrible, plus there's a lot of scientific stuff that I don't understand. But I've read enough to know that sometime in the 1980s his interest turned to the possibility of parallel universes and alternate dimensions."

"Wow, he really was out of his mind."

"Though they didn't exactly use those words, Dr. Canfield thought that was why the university fired him. When he informed them of the experiments he wanted to conduct, they let him go." Lucas flipped farther into the journal, stopped, and showed Simon a diagram.

"That's the big machine," Simon said, pointing to where it stood against the wall.

Dr. Canfield drew lines from each feature and scribbled in their purpose in tiny illegible script. "He began experiments using equipment he invented, like that."

After he found the journal, Lucas spent more time in the lab trying to decipher it. Early on Simon could pry him away so they could take the boat out on the lake, go fishing, shoot some hoops, or hike through the woods, but as time passed, it was harder to get him away from that old barn.

One day, just after summer vacation started, Lucas was scribbling his translation of what he took to calling the Canfield Journal and told Simon he had to finish the page before they'd ride their bikes into town. Simon went poking around the lab and found himself before that huge machine. He reached for the big switch.

"Don't," Lucas said.

Simon turned to him. "Huh? I'm just messing around."

"I think it still works." Lucas got up and joined him. "Look." Lucas grabbed the switch and pushed it halfway up. A humming started in the machine, the dials and gauges flickered, and small lights in them lit up. "Feel it?"

Simon held his hands toward the machine. "Yeah." Energy, like a barrier of static electricity, pulsed from the device. The little hairs on his body stood up. "What's it supposed to do?"

Lucas pulled the lever back and shut it down. "I don't know. I want to study the journal more before I push that switch all the way up."

"Probably a good idea."

Lucas pointed at the bottom of the machine around the right side. "Look at this." Coming out of the machine, multiple cables were tied together to form a six-inch diameter bundle that ran along the floor and out a hole in the wall. Lucas led him outside, and they followed the bundled cables through the woods to Dark Lake, where they disappeared into the water. "I got my snorkel gear and tried to follow it down, but it goes way deeper than I can go."

After that visit, Lucas got so obsessed with the Canfield Journal and the lab that Simon felt he wasn't much fun to be around, so he stopped going to Lakewood House.

Six weeks later, Simon got a phone call. "I know what the machine does."

"Lucas?" he asked, but Lucas had already hung up.

He considered going over to Lucas's right away, but Simon was going to meet some other kids on another part of the lake for a cookout. It wasn't until the next afternoon that Simon went to check on Lucas. He found Lucas in the barn, and he looked different. He'd lost a lot of weight in the last six weeks. His face was pale.

"I waited for you a long time," Lucas said. "But you never came."

"Sorry, I had something to do. I called you back, but you didn't answer."

Lucas swept his hand from left to right like he was wiping away the topic. "Doesn't matter. I got through most of Canfield's journal. I know what the machine is for."

"What?"

He grabbed Simon's forearm and looked at him intensely. "It opens a portal between our world and another in a parallel universe."

Simon stared a moment, then laughed. "Mad scientist, remember?"

Lucas didn't laugh. He didn't even smile.

"What's it connected to in the lake?" Simon asked.

Lucas nodded his approval of the question. "That's where the actual portal is, at the bottom of the lake."

"Why there?"

Lucas walked to the wall with the scorch marks. "This wasn't done by vandals. It was where Canfield put his first portal. When he tried to open it, it generated so much heat that it caught fire. He realized the only safe thing to do would be to put the portal in the lake, and the lake water would keep the temperature down."

"How would he know if it worked?" Lucas asked.

Lucas went to the machine. "If he got certain readings on the dials and meters, it meant the portal had opened." Lucas returned and put a hand on Simon's shoulder and whispered, "What he didn't know until later was that things were getting through when the portal opened."

"What things?"

"Animals—creatures—monsters."

Simon started to laugh, but the intensity in Lucas's gaze stopped him. "Monsters? Come on, Lucas."

Lucas grabbed the Canfield Journal and flipped to a page near the back. He held the journal out, and Simon took it. He gazed down on drawings that Canfield had made and realized these were supposed to be things that had come through the portal. Strange-looking creatures. One was a blob with dozens of little lines wiggling from it.

Lucas put his finger under the drawing. "Canfield called those lines cilia, hairlike growths that the creature used to move." His finger went to the next page, where Canfield had drawn another creature. Its head looked like a large serving bowl had been placed upside down. Canfield had drawn black dots running around the rim. Under the head were multiple limbs that ended in something like hands, though there were only three squarish fingers on each. The limbs it stood on had folded the fingers into fists. Lucas fingered the dots ringing its head. "He thought those were eyes, or some other type of sensory device, maybe something totally unknown to us."

Simon flipped through several more pages, each containing a picture of monsters Canfield claimed came through the portal in the lake and emerged on the shores of his property.

Lucas pointed at a creature that was skinny and tall. To Simon, it looked like an erect tapeworm. It was segmented, and the way the body bent and twisted, it didn't appear to have bones, though it stood upright. It was also the first of the creatures Simon had seen in the journal that had two arms and two legs.

"Canfield called that one the lurker." Lucas took a breath and added, "It's the one I saw." Simon turned to him so fast it's a wonder he didn't get whiplash. Lucas went on before he could respond. "I waited for you, and late last night, when you didn't come, I went ahead and flipped the switch on the machine fully on. I could feel energy coming from it. It hummed like before, but at a higher pitch. And then all the dials and meters went berserk, flashing and spinning. They finally settled on the same readings in the journal that Canfield said indicated the portal had been opened."

"And?"

"And I ran the machine for an hour before shutting it down."

"Come on, Lucas. Canfield was not sane. There are no monsters coming out of Dark Lake." Simon slammed the journal shut and shook it at Lucas. "All of this is bogus. None of the monsters in here are real."

Lucas didn't try to argue, but he said, "I went to the house after that. I walked into my room, and I saw the lurker in a shadow in the corner. I pretended I didn't see it so I wouldn't scare it away. In the journal, Canfield said he thought these creatures just wanted to observe him, observe our world. I studied it for a while from the corner of my eye while acting like I was getting ready for bed. Finally, when I was across the room, I looked at it directly. I couldn't see any eyes, but I definitely felt that it was, like Canfield said, observing me. I'm not sure how much time passed, fifteen minutes, twenty, and then I said, 'Hello.' And it was gone in an instant."

"Come on, Lucas. You don't really believe—"

Lucas grabbed the journal from Simon's hand and flipped to the back section. "There was only one that Canfield thought was dangerous. Here." He passed the journal back to Simon. Canfield had drawn this picture from above, kind of like if he'd taken a photo from up high with a drone. It showed Lakewood House's dock extending out into Dark Lake. At the end of the dock, in the water, two huge eyes gazed up. There was a giant shadow in the water, though its form was indistinct. "Canfield wrote that he saw it in the water several times and could feel menace coming from it. Though he never saw it out of the water, he did find an inch-thick layer of slime on the dock one morning. He theorized it was left by that creature when it came out of the water." Lucas put the journal in one of the desk drawers. "I don't believe Canfield moved away. I think that thing came out of Dark Lake and got him."

Simon couldn't think of how to respond. He was deeply worried about his friend. Not because of the things Lucas found in Canfield's journal; Simon was concerned with what he should do about Lucas. He seemed to be having a mental breakdown. Should he tell Lucas's parents? Ratting out a friend was definitely not something he wanted to do. But this was serious. As he rode his bike home, Simon decided he'd think about it overnight before making a decision.

It was shortly after dawn the following morning when Simon's phone woke him. It was Lucas's mother. "Simon, it's Mrs. King. Did Lucas stay at your house last night?"

"No, ma'am. He's not home?"

"No, Simon, and I'm so worried. He never came back to the house last night, and he's not at the barn. Did he say anything to you about going anywhere?"

"No, ma'am. I'll call around and see if anyone knows anything."

After they ended the call, Simon sat on the edge of his bed trying to figure out where Lucas might be. A terrible thought came to him. He jumped up and threw on the clothes he'd worn the day before. A few minutes after that he was on his bike racing to Lakewood House. He bypassed the house and leaped off his bike as he got to the lake. He stood there, mouth open, as the morning sun sparkled and reflected off a thick layer of slime that coated the dock.

Simon ran to the barn and took out the journal from its hiding place in the drawer and flipped through it to the pictures. A piece of paper fell from the pages. Simon unfolded it and read.

Simon,

If something happens to me, it's because I made a big mistake while trying to translate the Canfield Journal. His handwriting is so bad that I missed something important. I went back over instructions on running the machine and saw I'd missed a step. When I turned it on and ran it that first time, it only opened the portal. To close it, I needed to run the machine a second time. So I tried, but something in the machine broke, and it will no longer turn on. I've been hearing something in the lake, something really big, splashing around, making strange sounds, and I'm scared. I'm going to try to make it to the house.

In a state of shock, Simon looked up from the note and gazed out blankly. Something caught his attention from the corner of his eye. He turned to the dark corner past the scorched wall, where the lurker stood and observed him.

CHAPTER 8

THE HOUSE OF MYSTERY AND MIRRORS (PART 2)

Jana and I sat and stared at each other, our eyes wide and round. We knew the stories, we recorded the telling of them, but for some reason, tonight, it was like we were hearing them for the first time, and they were both spell-binding and terrifying. Maybe it was because it was after dark, or maybe it was because it was Halloween night, but I had the feeling that much more than mere stories was at play.

Jana realized there was only silence on our podcast,

what's known as *dead air*. An appropriate term to use tonight. She started playing the intro to the "House of Mystery and Mirrors," that awful calliope music. I was about to go back to the other side of the mirrors, at least in my mind and in my telling.

If I thought too much about it, I might have a difficult time starting, so I just opened my mouth and said, "Welcome back to my portion of tonight's *Odd Occurrences*. I'll try to share what happened in a way that makes sense. I can't promise anything, because that'll be attempting to make the irrational sound rational, the impossible sound plausible, the supernatural sound real."

We stepped through the mirror and exited the maze into what we could only assume was the house part of the House of Mystery and Mirrors. Next to the mirror was an old suit of armor like knights wore. The helmet was held in the crook of one of the arms. Rising from the chest plate of the stone knight was a skull that had turned brownish-yellow with age.

Once in the hallway, we looked back at the mirror. Tobin reached toward it and pushed his hand through the mirror surface. "The portal opens both ways."

"Come on. Let's find the door and get out."

Just as the exterior of the House of Mystery and Mirrors was black, so was the interior, though it wasn't paint. There was wallpaper in the hall and some rooms; others were painted in what might have once been bright hues. But now the walls, the ceilings, the floors, and much of the furnishings were tinged with a black residue, mold perhaps, or maybe smoke stains from the gas lamps that burned everywhere.

We walked a couple dozen feet, and the hallway intersected with another. Both extended a great distance, but none were straight. They curved either left or right, and we couldn't see where the hallways ended. Shadowed recesses indicated where doors to rooms were. Paintings hung on the walls, but the black residue changed what they depicted. Landscapes resembled paintings of hell, and portraits looked like monsters. There were more suits of armor in the hallways, as well as statues, though the marble appeared soot-stained.

Some of the doors off the hallway were open and some were closed, but none of them were locked. We looked into each we passed. There were a lot of bedrooms, as well as a library, and what looked like an office of sorts, with old-fashioned filing cabinets, an office desk the size of a Ping-Pong table, and an office lamp with a green glass lampshade.

"You know what every room is missing?" I asked.

"Windows. Which is weird, since we saw a lot of windows when we were outside the house," Tobin said. He paused and then asked, "Hear that?"

I stood still and held my breath. A low thumping was coming from farther down the hall.

"Is it a machine or something?" I asked.

"Sounds like a heartbeat."

We followed the passage for a long time, finally coming to where it ended at two closed doors. I took the knob on the right side, an oversized brass ball, tarnished and dull. Tobin took the matching knob on the other, and we opened both doors into a massive, circular room, at least fifty feet across. Twin doors, like the one we stood at, were at even intervals in the walls.

"I hate to tell you this, Zeus."

"What?"

"Counting ours, there are thirteen entrances to this room."

I groaned. "Of course there are."

The ceiling mushroomed into a dome shape, and a mural had been painted on it. My best guess was that it had originally depicted angels, cherubs, and seraphim flying overhead and observing the goings-on below. Now, with the black stippling of mold, or smoke, or whatever, it looked more like dead creatures emerging from the muck of a swamp.

The room was empty, except for a ten-foot-tall mound of clothes to the side and a canvas-covered object in the center. It was eight feet high and three feet wide, and the throbbing emanated from it.

"I want to see what's under the drop cloth," Tobin said.

I nodded and we started for it, but we didn't get ten steps before we stopped. The closer we got, the more we could feel its rhythmic pulse in our chests. It wasn't a good feeling. I took one more step forward and began to feel a little sick to my stomach.

"On second thought, let's not," I said.

Tobin nodded, and we retreated to the circular wall and made our way to the next set of doors and went through.

We walked the halls and explored rooms for a long time. I tried to keep cool; I didn't want Tobin to know I was panicking on the inside. Lost in a mirror maze was one thing, but wandering around inside an impossible house meant that something far beyond normal was at play.

"The House of Mystery and Mirrors is like those tents back at the carnival," Tobin said. "Bigger on the inside than the outside."

"But on a much larger scale." My mind struggled to come up with a comparison. "This is like taking an NFL football stadium and cramming it into a storage shed."

The corridor we walked ended in a foyer that included a wide staircase leading to an upper floor. Numerous passages led from the lobby like tunnels in an ant colony.

Tobin looked around and pointed to the stairs. "Let's go up there. Might find some windows or see something that tells us where we are." By the tremor in his voice, I knew he was as close to panic as me.

We ascended the stairs, chose one of a dozen hallways, and ventured in.

"None of this makes any sense," I said.

"Nope." He lifted his head when an idea came to him. "Do you think they hypnotized us? You know, giving us the ultimate carnival experience."

I thought about it. "No. I think something bad has happened to us, and it's only going to get worse."

Tobin stopped and grabbed my arm. "Listen." In the distance came the repetitive slap of someone running in sneakers. The sound echoed in the corridors. "Someone else is here."

We ran toward the sound, and way down the hall, coming from around a curve, Vince and Nash appeared, running toward us. Vince saw us and started gesturing with his arm.

"What's he doing?" Tobin asked.

"I think he's signaling us to get out of here."

They reached a point where the hallway intersected with another, from which two figures charged. One was tremendously big.

"Big Guy," Tobin whispered.

He carried his massive sledgehammer in one hand and grabbed Nash with his other. Nash screamed shrilly. The other figure, easily recognizable by two heads on one body, tackled Vince. As he—they—hauled Vince to his feet, I immediately recognized that Winston and Hume had dressed like hunters on a safari. Their body wore tan slacks tucked into high lace-up boots, and a matching button-down shirt. Hume sported a white pith helmet, and Winston had on a leather hat, similar to a flat-topped cowboy hat, except that one side was pinned up to the crown.

We were so stunned we couldn't move. Tobin snapped out of it first, grabbed me, and pulled me back through a door into a room.

"What the heck was that about?" I whispered.

Tobin shook his head.

Cautiously, we peeked into the hallway.

Vince and Nash continued to struggle as a new figure appeared, gliding over the floor, and she inspired more screams from Vince and Nash. Tall and thin, her pale flesh mottled with black smudges, she looked like a ghost.

That was it; any shred of self-control fled, and Tobin and I ran for another door at the far end of the room. It opened into another corridor, and we ran for all we were worth. I was behind Tobin and tried to keep up as he made random turns. Right into this hallway, left through this antechamber, straight up that passageway.

Wheezing, I stumbled to a stop. "Wait," I croaked.

Tobin looked back and then returned.

Winded, I sat on the floor. "I think we're good. Let's catch our breath."

Panting, he nodded.

"What was that thing with Winston, Hume, and Big Guy?" I asked after I caught my breath.

Tobin shook his head. "Ghost? Monster? Demon? Something that wasn't human."

I got to my feet. "Which way?"

"Does it matter?" Tobin started in the direction we'd been running.

I followed, and soon we found ourselves approaching a once-elegant staircase leading down. Tobin got to the landing first and put out a hand to stop me. He put a finger to his lips and pointed. Someone sat midway down, their back to us. They had long white hair and were hunched over. We started to back away from the edge, hoping not to be noticed.

The person turned their head to us and smiled weakly. "Hello. Could you help an old man up the staircase?"

It was the Oracle.

We holed up with the Oracle in a bedroom suite on the fourth floor of the house. Apparently bigger inside than out worked vertically as well as horizontally when it came to the House of Mystery and Mirrors.

Tobin collapsed onto a four-poster bed ringed with mesh curtains that had been tied open. I sat on the floor, leaning back against the wall. The Oracle groaned as he sat on an old-fashioned leather sofa.

He cleared his throat and began our education. "The reality that we are in is the House of Mystery and Mirrors. It can be broken into two areas, the maze and the house. If you go through the portal mirror into the maze, you're still in the house. However, if you go through the portal mirror into the house, you've left the mirrors."

"That doesn't make sense," Tobin barked.

The Oracle smiled. "Exactly. And the sooner you realize that none of it makes sense, the longer you can survive." He'd worn his oracle robe at the carnival, but here he had on a faded New York Jets T-shirt and washed-out jeans. It was odd to see someone so old in high-top sneakers. "Time doesn't matter here. As long as you think you've been here—"

"A few hours," Tobin interrupted.

"If you were to somehow make your way back, you'd find that only a second had passed in the real world, or it could be a year. Because time doesn't matter here, you won't ever be hungry, which is good, because there's no food. You'll never be thirsty, and you'll never sleep. The only thing you need to concern yourself with now, and for the rest of your life, is to not be taken."

I told him about what we'd seen happen to Vince and Nash. "Is that what you mean by taken?"

The Oracle nodded.

"Were they killed?" Tobin asked.

"No, they aren't dead. But if you see them again, they'll be twenty years older, maybe thirty or more depending on how long they had to stand before the Black Mirror." He saw our confusion. "My name is Billy Ellis. Seems odd to call an old man Billy, doesn't it?"

Tobin shrugged.

He laughed, and it sounded like sandpaper rubbing wood. "But you can call me Kid."

I wondered if he suffered from dementia. "Kid?"

"I'm only fifteen years old." He saw our expressions and nodded to emphasize what he said. "I walked the maze five months ago. I've been taken by The Exceptionals to the Domed Chamber, and this is the result." He pointed at his face.

"I think we went through there," I said. "A huge round room, dome ceiling, thirteen doors, and something under canvas in the middle of the room."

"The Black Mirror is under the canvas. I've stood before

it three times, and I am now old. Once more and I'll die." He scratched at his beard. "It's inevitable." He looked from me to Tobin and held up a shaky hand. "I know, I know. It sounds unbelievable. But listen and I'll try to explain it. The Queen of the Carnival is not human. And the beautiful woman she presents herself to be in the world we come from is not what she truly looks like. You saw her true shape when they took those kids. You say their names are Vince and Nash, right?"

"Yeah," I said, numbly. "So you're saying that thing was the Queen, and that's what she really looks like?"

"That's what she is. A parasite. She wears a disguise in our world. Maybe *wear* isn't the right word. She transforms herself. It takes a lot of power for that transformation, and it takes even more to be the Queen and to maintain the House of Mystery and Mirrors. The Exceptionals are her army. In a way, they worship her. In her travels all over the world, she has collected them and used her powers to influence them to do her bidding. She's good at what she does because she's been doing it for centuries. She's that old."

I pointed at him. "You were working at the carnival, but you're not an Exceptional."

"Sometimes they'll take us out of the mirrors to work.

But only if we're old and slow and can't run away. I'm not really an oracle. My job was to steer kids to the House of Mystery and Mirrors."

Tobin's expression tightened. He sat up and swung his legs off the bed. He was on the verge of losing his temper. "You sent kids here? To this place?"

Kid hung his head. "I didn't want to. They made me do it."

"Just following orders," Tobin snorted.

Looking at the floor, Kid shook his head. "I know, I know. But being out there in the real world again, even as an old man, even if I couldn't leave the carnival, was wonderful. I did what they asked so I could be out there." He quickly glanced up at us. "But not for long. If you'll remember, I gave you a note, written with my blood, to get out, to leave the carnival. I did that because you helped me with those jerks. It's not my fault you didn't follow my advice. Just like it's not your fault that Falstaff caught me trying to help you and made me walk the maze again."

Tobin sighed and sat back against the headboard. "He knew you tried to help us?"

"Yes. Those you saw take Vince and Nash brought me with them when they came to hunt. If you're wondering why they didn't just take me to the Black Mirror, it's because they enjoy hunting."

"That means you've been through the maze three times, twice in and once out. Do you think you can find your way out again?" I asked.

"Get real," Kid said. "You could go through a hundred times, and you'd still get lost. You'd need a map to make it through. And then you'd have to hope you didn't run into any Exceptionals on the way."

"Why do they do it? Why did they kidnap Tobin and me?"

"That's the true purpose of the carnival, to travel the world and take kids."

"Why kids?" Tobin asked.

Kid pursed his lips in thought and then said, "I'll use a vampire analogy. Instead of blood, the Queen eats years. She consumes life, energy, youth. They only trick kids into the mirrors because kids have the greatest amount of youth. A kid can be taken several times, whereas an adult could only be taken once, maybe twice. The youthful energy wouldn't be as potent. When they take a kid to the Domed Chamber, the Black Mirror drains that youth and energy and life, and it leaves them older. Get taken three or four times and it's ashes to ashes, dust to dust, literally. On the flip side of that coin, the life force taken from us feeds the Queen and keeps her strong and gives her immortality. In turn, she uses her power to offer The Exceptionals unending life. And without her power, they would cease to exist, as would the House of Mystery and Mirrors."

"Does it hurt?" Tobin asked quietly. "You know, when they take you?"

Kid snapped, "Of course it hurts! They're taking a major part of your youth, decades of your life! It's like having a limb amputated without anesthesia!" He took deep breaths, calming himself. "I was here for a long time before they first took me. It's like the most serious round of hide-and-seek you can imagine. I thought my hiding place was good, but they still found me."

Tobin stood and started pacing. "What happens when you get taken to the Black Mirror?"

Kid looked at him a moment. "Just hope that you never find out."

"What's with all the black stuff covering everything?" I asked. "Is it mold or soot?"

"I have a theory. The house is bad; it's putrid, and everything in it is in a state of decay. The black substance that covers everything is rot."

We were quiet for a minute as we thought that over. Finally, I said, "My parents will be looking for me. Tobin's too."

Kid smiled sadly. "No, they won't. No one misses any of the kids in here. No one will search for them. Nobody will search for you."

"I don't understand."

"When I was out there, telling fortunes, that's when I learned how long I'd been in here. I saw a newspaper and checked the date. I'd been in here five months. Anyway, a woman left her purse in my tent. I went through it and found her cell phone. I got lucky. I swiped the screen and it opened; she didn't use a PIN number. I called my parents." His lips trembled. "They didn't know me. They thought I was a prank call and hung up. I called my sister at college, and she didn't know me, either. I called my best friend, and he didn't remember me." Kid rubbed his face. "When you're in the mirrors, you're forgotten out there. When they take me to the Black Mirror for the final time, it will be as if I never existed, and no one will mourn."

In the dimly lit existence of endless hallways, Tobin and I and an ancient fifteen-year-old survived. Ninety-nine percent of the time it was boring inside the mirrors. The other 1 percent was pure adrenaline-fueled terror.

When we'd been there for what seemed like a few days, we once again talked about the possibility of finding a door out.

Tobin grumbled, "Heck with a door, I can't believe there aren't any windows in this stupid house."

"You want to see out?" Kid asked.

"Of course."

Kid led us up, navigating hallways and rooms and climbing staircases, which we had to help him up. We passed a number of kids along the way, and kids who looked like adults and senior citizens. Some had given up and walked the halls with glazed eyes, waiting for The Exceptionals to take them. Others we stopped to talk with, exchange information, and get any news about the outside world.

There was a limit as to how high the House of Mystery and Mirrors rose. On the inside, the house contained twelve stories. On the twelfth floor, Kid led us up and down a few hallways and stopped at a narrow door. It squeaked loudly when he opened it to a set of wooden steps. All the other staircases we had climbed had been ornately built. This one was simple old wood. The steps hadn't even been sanded, and you'd run the risk of big splinters going up barefooted. We followed it up into an attic. Compared with the rest of the house, it was small, maybe twenty feet by twenty. The ceiling was the underside of the roof and sloped. I could walk standing straight up if I went down the center, but I had to bend over if I went to either side.

"There," Kid said. "That's the only way to look out." He pointed at the attic vent.

Tobin and I ran to the octagonal-shaped vent, which was a little bigger than a basketball. We peered down through horizontal wooden slats to the front yard of the House of Mystery and Mirrors, and the buzzing streetlight just beyond that. All of it surrounded by woods and the dark of night.

My mind did the math. "Okay, so we're in the attic of a twelve-story house."

"Meaning we're on the thirteenth floor," Tobin added.

I grimaced at the unlucky number but returned to my point. "So we should be a hundred and thirty to a hundred and fifty feet up."

"But it's like we're looking out of the attic of a two-story house," Tobin finished my thought.

Kid shrugged. "Maybe it has to do with the impossible physics of being bigger inside than out. Since we're looking out, the view is that of a two-story house."

As much as I didn't want to hang out on the thirteenth floor, we set up a headquarters of sorts, a place to while away the time. From the attic vent, we could keep a watch on the front of the house. We took shifts there so we'd know when The Exceptionals came to hunt. Like Kid said, and from what we observed, they enjoyed hunting as much for sport as they did for survival. In a way, the House of Mystery and Mirrors was a big-game preserve, and we were the game. The Domed Chamber was the trophy room, where those they'd taken had to face the Black Mirror.

We developed a strategy to survive when The Exceptionals came for victims, and it served us well for a good number of hunts. Tobin and I explored all the rooms close to the attic door, and we constructed a hiding place of sorts in one of the suites. There was a fireplace in a wall that separated a sitting room from a bedroom, and it opened to both rooms. Other than the mantels above and the fireplace tools, neither side would look like a fireplace if covered. We stashed the fireplace tools in other rooms. On the mantel in the sitting room, we placed a large painting, hoping it would look like that was the mantel's purpose. We gathered a bunch of small statues and figurines and placed them on the mantel in the bedroom.

To hide the fireplace in the bedroom, we pushed a chest of drawers in front of it. In the sitting room, we hid the fireplace behind a writing bureau. It had three wide drawers in the bottom half. The front of the upper half could be pulled down to provide a desk for writing. The fireplace was big enough that the three of us could fit in it snugly. The writing bureau was pretty heavy, but once we were all in the fireplace, Tobin and I could move it into place if we worked together.

Dozens, if not hundreds, of kids were in the house with us. Most stayed in small groups, and some preferred being on their own, though we often met up in the hallways. Carnival Nocturne traveled the globe and took kids from every corner of the world. So not everyone spoke the same language. Before Carnival Nocturne came to Crescent Harbor, it'd made several other Florida stops, including in St. Augustine, where the Florida School for the Deaf and Blind is located. Two girls who had been students there now walked the maze, and because of them, we added a little sign language to our communication, including how to sign "good luck" and, more important, how to sign "run."

We did talk to Vince and Nash now and again. The first time, they both looked like they were in their midthirties, though they were just as immature as before. The last we saw of Nash, he looked like he was in his sixties. He was mad because when The Exceptionals cornered them in a large suite, Vince had escaped out another door, leaving Nash to get taken.

A lot of different Exceptionals took part in the hunts, and Tobin, being Tobin, gave some of them names as we watched them approach the house from above. There was Gill Man, Squish Boy, Inside-Out Girl, Centipede, Reptile Twins, and Lady Squid. It seemed important to know as much as possible about our enemy, so I drew them in my sketch pad.

We took shifts watching for The Exceptionals, but that didn't mean we always stayed in the attic. That would drive a person insane. So, when one was on lookout duty, the others would sometimes go explore. Kid couldn't go far, but even he liked to get out of the attic and stretch his legs. Tobin and I, on the other hand, liked to get out and explore for hours at a time, sometimes together and sometimes on our own. While we learned our way around the general vicinity of the attic and several floors below, when we went really far from the attic, I'd draw maps in the sketchbook so we could easily find our way back. It was while working on a map of the fourth floor that I had an idea. I remembered Kid telling us that the only way someone could find their way through the maze of mirrors was if they had a map. I began to work on one.

We'd long since found the route to the portal mirror on the first floor. When I wasn't on lookout duty, I'd work my way into the maze, making sure I always mapped where I'd been so I wouldn't get lost again. I'd start out in one direction, noting each turn, whether I took it or not. It was slow, tedious work, but I began to feel optimistic because I thought I'd correctly mapped out at least one one-hundredth of the mirror maze. That's not a lot, but it meant it was possible. I could spend more time in the maze, see if I could speed things up. I could also teach Tobin how to do it, and that would double the map's progress.

I brought it up with Tobin and Kid.

"Ah man, what I wouldn't give to feel the sun on my skin again," Tobin said.

"I can take longer shifts at the vent, give you two more time to make the map," Kid volunteered.

At this point, it felt like Tobin and I had been in the house for at least half a year. We had a major setback before Tobin could even begin to help with the map.

I'd been in the mirrors with my sketch pad, double-checking a route I'd mapped out earlier. I heard something in the distance. I stood motionless and caught someone saying something. Though I didn't understand what she said, I recognized the Queen's voice. They were on the hunt.

I took a second to return my sketchbook to my backpack and then ran. I should have probably gone slower and tried to run silently, but I panicked, and I think they heard my footsteps.

As I passed through the portal mirror, I heard a deep, croaking voice: "There's one ahead."

I had to get to the twelfth floor and our hiding spot, but I had to make sure they weren't close behind me. If they followed me to that specific part of the house, that meant there'd be more of a chance for them to find the hidden fireplace. As I ascended higher into the house, I'd occasionally stop and listen. Each time I heard a ping sound, like someone tapping a resonant piece of metal with a small hammer. The pinging would repeat every several seconds. I didn't know what it was, but I did know I wasn't losing them. They always seemed to be close behind. As I ran up a staircase to the tenth floor, I decided that I couldn't get to the hiding spot far enough ahead of them. For the sake of Tobin and Kid, I'd have to lead them away and hope they got some other poor kid before they got me.

Just as I made the landing, Tobin rounded a corner at full speed. "Zeus, they're on the hunt!"

"I know, they're right behind me."

Tobin's eyes grew wide, and he motioned me to follow. Around the corner Kid came at us at a hobbling run.

I was mad. "Why didn't you guys go to the hiding spot?"

"Because we came to get you."

I hiked a thumb over my shoulder. "They're tracking me. I think they'd find us if we went to the fireplace now. We'll have to try to outrun them."

We ran with Kid between us, his arms over our shoulders. Kid tried to run with us, but the more exhausted he got, the more he stumbled. We dashed through a suite of rooms and exited another door into a different hallway and took a left. Kid lurched toward me and his right foot tangled with my left ankle, and then somehow his left ankle got caught between Tobin's legs, and we all went down hard. Tobin and I jumped up, took Kid's arms, and lifted him.

Kid shook his head and wheezed. "I can't."

I nodded to a nearby intersection, and Tobin and I

dragged him there. We sat him down just around the corner with his back against the wall. The way he was wheezing scared me. Tobin kept watch around the corner and then gave me a look that said we should get going.

I put my hand on Kid's shoulder. "Ready?"

Kid shook his head and, between breaths, said, "Can't. Go—without me."

"They're hunting," Tobin said. "You can't let them take you again."

"I'm too old," Kid said.

"You're fifteen," I said.

Kid produced a dry laugh and rubbed his wrinkled face. "I was born fifteen years ago." He held up his hands and looked at them. "But I'm—so—old."

"We gotta go," Tobin whispered to me.

"Are they here?"

"No, but they will be."

"Just one more minute," I said. It was the least we could do, give up sixty seconds of lead so Kid could catch his breath.

Kid's lungs rattled. "If I could have anything right now, it would be an hour back home on a Sunday afternoon."

I took his hand. "Yeah?"

"Mom and I would sit on our back porch and laugh while

our hundred-and-twenty-pound mastiff, Bongo, wrestled my little sister, who's so small everybody calls her Flea. We'd laugh so hard we'd have to lean against each other to stay sitting up. Dad would be laughing, too, but over by the grill." Kid coughed weakly. "He always fires up the grill on Sundays. But not burgers, oh no. Stuff like standing rib roast, or a chicken that had spent hours in his secret cilantro chipotle marinade, or baby back ribs with his special dry rub mix. Mom would make dessert. And if we were really lucky, we'd catch the scent of cinnamon through the open kitchen window as it cooked." Kid's breathing was shallow, and he stared out with glazed eyes. "That meant she was making her apple cobbler." His leathered lips spread in a smile and he stopped moving.

Tobin studied him, and his voice broke when he whispered, "Is Kid dead?"

"No. He's just up here," I said, and tapped the side of my head. "Remembering better times." I stood. "He can't run anymore. Let's backtrack and then head off in another direction. They'll track us and won't find him."

We ran back up the hallway past the suite door we'd exited, Tobin pulling ahead. Another hallway broke to the left, and Tobin paused there to let me catch up.

He looked past me and said, "Oh no."

I pushed Tobin into the left-hand hall. We peeked around the corner to see the three Exceptionals follow the route we'd taken through the suite. Manther came through the door first on hands and feet. His head swung one way and then the other, settling his attention up the hallway. Frog Boy hopped out next and looked our way. We pulled our heads back around the corner.

"Wait. I will tell you which way they went." Though we couldn't see her, I recognized the voice of the Queen of the Carnival. The pinging started again, and I risked a glance. Frog Boy's attention was no longer focused in our direction but up at her. Being closer, we had a better look at her appearance on this side of the mirrors. She was gaunt and tall, with translucent skin like a slug's belly. Around her eyes, nostrils, and mouth, it looked as if she had powdered her flesh with coal dust. She opened and closed her mouth repeatedly and wide, exposing her black mouth and tongue. I realized she was tracking us with echolocation.

Retreating back around the corner, Tobin whispered, "Should we go?"

"I don't know. If her echolocation works around corners, we'd be toast."

Tobin looked at me with a confused expression, and another ping sounded. "Is that what she's doing? Echolocation? Like a bat?"

I nodded. "Like sonar. I think that's how she's tracking us."

Tobin moved slowly, putting his left eye past the corner. "Oh man, look."

I peeked to see that Kid had gotten to his feet and was stumbling toward the trio of hunters.

Frog Boy was the first to see him and called out in a bass croak, "Over there."

Manther shot down the hallway, bounding from wall to wall, and hurled himself at Kid, knocking him to the floor. A second later the Queen and Frog Boy stood over him. She held out a hand, her fingers twitching, and Kid stood. The Exceptionals started off in the opposite direction. Blank-eyed, Kid followed, walking with as much awkwardness as a zombie in a B movie.

"He sacrificed himself," I whispered.

"He saved us." Tobin started around the corner, wanting to go help him.

I grabbed his wrist and pulled him back. "There's nothing we can do."

"They're taking him to the Domed Chamber," Tobin growled, and tried to pull free. I gripped him harder, looked him in the eye, and shook my head.

We stared at each other for several seconds, and then he nodded.

I sat, back against the wall, thinking how Tobin and I had survived another hunt. Then I thought how The Exceptionals would drain the rest of Kid's life and return to our world like it was no big deal. An idea grew in my mind. I thought on it. Was it foolhardy? Yeah. Was there a chance? Maybe.

"I have a plan. Let's follow them through the maze."

Tobin looked at me through narrowed eyes. "First, we'd have to follow them to the Domed Chamber."

"Yep."

"And then we'd have to monitor them in the Domed Chamber so we'll know which door they leave by."

"Yeah."

"In the maze, we'll have to follow at a distance so they don't see us in a reflection. There's a chance we'd lose them."

"A good chance."

"They could notice us following them at any time."

I nodded. "Uh-huh."

He inhaled deeply. "But there's no other chance of getting out, is there?"

"Nope." I stood and put my hands on Tobin's shoulders. "But only if you think it's worth the risk."

He gave a lopsided grin. "Let's go home."

Following the Queen and her Exceptionals to the Domed Chamber turned out to be easy. Thanks to all our exploration, we knew the quickest route there, so we didn't have to follow them closely. We made it to the first floor and heard the familiar throbbing from the Black Mirror. Rounding a corner, we were a good distance away as they entered the Domed Chamber and closed the double doors behind them.

I know Tobin wanted to help Kid. I did, too, but we faced the fact that it would be a futile gesture that would put us all before the Black Mirror. Kid would be none the better for it. A minute later Kid started screaming. We got to the door when he stopped and cracked it open just as Manther threw the canvas cloth back over the mirror. There was no sign of Kid other than empty clothes on the floor and ashy powder swirling to the ground. They had taken him for the last time, reducing his body to dust.

Manther tossed the jeans, T-shirt, and shoes onto the tall pile of discarded clothes. They headed for a doorway across the chamber. When those doors closed, we hurried across the room, trying to ignore the bad feelings that emanated from the Black Mirror.

Tobin reached for the door.

"Wait a second." I pulled off my backpack and got out my sketchpad and a charcoal pencil.

"What are you doing?" Tobin whispered.

"I'm going to finish the map."

He looked at me, brows creased, and then shrugged and opened one of the doors.

Once we passed through the portal mirror, I let Tobin take the lead while I worked on the map. We kept back, following by sound. Though they occasionally spoke, the Queen was mostly silent as she glided through the maze. Manther was quiet as well, but hearing the sound of Frog Boy hopping and landing on his belly with an accompanying croak was almost as good as following them by sight.

We took the labyrinth in reverse, staying just out of sight of The Exceptionals and working hard at not making a sound. In fact, the most noise we made was my charcoal pencil scratching the map into the sketchbook. We trudged through the part of the maze with all the different shapes and sizes of mirrors. I worried that the Queen would see us in a wayward reflection, so we dropped back some more.

It was amazing how quickly we were getting through. Tobin and I had spent hours in the maze, but now, trailing The Exceptionals, I estimated we'd be out in ten minutes, fifteen at the most. Surprisingly, working on the map hadn't slowed us down, and I felt I was getting the route accurately.

Tobin put a hand on my arm and put his mouth close to my ear. "Let's give them a little more lead time."

I nodded, and we waited a minute before starting up again. Tobin was eight feet in front of me, and I looked down as I drew in a right turn at a corridor three intersections past our last turn.

"Uh-oh," Tobin mumbled.

I looked up to see Tobin stopped at a T-intersection. We could go either left or right. We heard The Exceptionals, but the way sound bounced around the mirrors, the noise could have come from either direction. We heard a door close and then no noise at all.

"I think they're out," Tobin said. "We're close, Zeus."

"I know. But which way?"

Tobin looked from left to right and back again. "You go left; I'll go right."

"What? No. We stick together."

"If we pick wrong, we could end up lost in the maze again," Tobin said.

"And if we split up, one of us will definitely be lost."

Tobin looked at me and grinned. "You are so smart, dude. I thought it was a waste of time for you to keep working on the map, but not now. If I get out and you're still in, use your map to get back to this spot and take the other way. I'll wait for you outside the House of Mystery and Mirrors. If you get out, mark it on the map, and then use it to come back and find me."

I grinned. It would work. We were going to get out of the mirrors. Tobin and I shook with a bro handshake, and then he went right and I went left. Ten feet later, I had to take a right, then a left, and I found myself facing the front door of the House of Mystery and Mirrors. I started to go back after Tobin but decided to first make sure the coast was clear. I opened the door and stepped onto the porch, and everything went black.

I made a slashing gesture in front of my throat to indicate to Jana that I was ready to cut away from my narration. She quickly brought up our theme music, and I mouthed, *Thank you*. Even though I was just relaying what had happened in the past, it still unnerved me, and at times it still frightened me. I needed a moment to compose myself, which Jana recognized, and she took over.

"We'll take a break from House of Mystery and Mirrors and let Zeus catch his breath. In the meantime, we have more Odd Occurrences coming up, including what happens to a girl suffering from pediophobia. An anonymous caller with a stutter relayed how a game led to an encounter with a serial killer. We've got one that will make you question whether our reality is real, and we'll start now with how painting graffiti on a train turned into a supernatural nightmare."

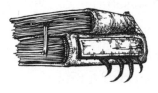

CHAPTER 9

EMPEROR BULL

She wanted to be a writer. Not like a book writer or a newspaper writer. She wanted to be a writer as in a graffiti artist. Her brother was almost twenty, and he'd been putting up tags and pieces for years. She asked him to teach her, but he said that she wasn't an artist and that girls couldn't do it as well. That was one thing about her: If you told her she couldn't do something, she'd want to do it that much more. If you told her she couldn't do something because she was a girl, she'd do it with a passion. She had this fantasy of people sitting at a railroad crossing waiting for a train to go by, and they'd see the tag, Squatch13, on a freight car or on the undercarriage.

That'd be hers. Squatch was her writer's name, thirteen because that's how old she was. Her tag would include a Sasquatch on a skateboard.

That night, she was in the yard where they keep all the train cars that aren't running. She had a backpack full of cannons clanking around—you know, spray paint cans. She was working on her first big piece, lots of crazy shapes that joined together like jigsaw puzzle pieces. She had laid out the outline the night before on an autorack, a freight car that is long, flat, and tall. It was a good distance from the yard's security office. Tonight, she was going to color in all those puzzle pieces. Up close, it'd look great, but at a distance, you'd see the shape of a man with his arms outstretched. And of course, her tag, Squatch13, would be underneath. That was the plan, but something happened before she started the color.

Squatch laid out all her cannons in a row on the ground in front of the train car. She'd shaken them before she got to the yard because those metal mixing balls banging around in paint cans are loud. She'd brought her dad's old wooden ladder the night before, and she pulled it out from under the car where she'd stashed it and put it up. Holding one spray paint can, she backed up ten yards to look at what she'd already painted.

That's when the fog blew in. It was unreal; one second it wasn't there, the next second it was swirling past, and the second after that it was so foggy she couldn't see the cannons, the ladder, or even the freight car. The temperature dropped from warm to chilly, and it seemed like the mist reached out to stroke her face with wet fingers. She looked one way and then the other, turned around, and then back in what she thought was the direction she'd been facing. She took one slow step after another, trying to get back to the freight car, but when she'd gone on for too long without finding it, she knew she'd wandered the wrong way.

In the dark and fog, Squatch heard footsteps. It was more than one person, and they were running straight toward her. She brought up her can of Montana Brand Vivid Red spray paint as if that would protect her. A second later she was slammed by someone big and went flying. Squatch landed on her back, the can of paint rolling from her hand. The running stopped, and someone grabbed a handful of her hoodie and lifted her to her feet. She blinked several times at the three men standing there.

"You hurt?" the biggest one, the one who ran into her, asked. He wore overalls and looked like a farmer. He had a flat wool cap on his head and a stuffed burlap sack over his shoulder.

She took a moment to see how she felt. A little bruised was all. "I'm okay."

"Come on, Okra Joe, we gotta go," the smallest of the men said. He looked like he'd been wearing a business-man's suit and hat for five years without ever taking them off. In fact, all the men wore clothes that were dirty and frayed, and she could smell perspiration and body odor.

"Just makin' sure this kid's all right, Shoeless."

Sure enough, the guy in the suit was barefoot. His feet black with dirt. "Ah, the bo-ette is just a preshun."

Squatch was starting to get mad. "What's that?"

"A girl punk," Shoeless said.

The third man pushed Shoeless away. His skin was al-most as dark as hers, and he wore a flannel shirt missing several buttons. Canvas pants were held up with a belt made from a length of rope. He had a thick stick over his shoulder, and at the end was a red-and-white bandanna with all four corners tied around it, bulging with his be-longings. He put a hand to his chest. "Some people call us bums or tramps, or since we jump trains, hobos." He bent over to look her in the eye. "A bo-ette is a girl hobo, but I prefer the term *rail rider*, so you're a girl rail rider.

A preshun means a rail kid, new to the nomadic life. I'm Cabbage Patch. What's your moniker, kid?"

"My what?"

"Your rail rider name."

They all had such strange ones—Okra Joe, Shoeless, Cabbage Patch—so she gave them her writer's name. "I'm Squatch."

The big one, Okra Joe, looked down at her. "Emperor Bull is out tonight. You best hit the skids."

It was then that she noticed all three were frightened. "Who's Emperor Bull?"

"This kid is green," Shoeless said.

"A bull is a railroad security man, and Emperor Bull is the biggest and meanest of 'em all," Cabbage Patch said. "Whatcha doin' out here tonight, Squatch?"

"Writing."

"Writing?"

"You know, graffiti."

"Graffiti?" Cabbage Patch said, and by their expressions, she could tell none of them had a clue as to what she meant.

"Painting pictures on a freight car."

"Ohhhh," Okra Joe said. "Leaving your mark."

"Come on, guys. We gotta get out of here." Shoeless

was jumping from one foot to the other like a little kid who had to use the bathroom.

"Using chalk?" Cabbage Patch asked.

"Huh? No." Squatch took a moment to find her cannon and held it up. "Spray paint." Once again, all three had blank expressions.

She picked up a piece of wood and shook the can, the metal mixing ball inside it rattling.

Cabbage Patch grabbed her wrist and stilled it. "Shhhh. You can't make that kinda racket with Emperor Bull around."

She aimed the can at the wood and sprayed it red.

"Will wonders never cease," Cabbage Patch said.

Shoeless whispered forcefully, "Who cares. We gotta go before Emperor Bull shows."

Okra Joe nodded and walked into the fog, Shoeless behind him, and they vanished.

Cabbage Patch put a hand on her shoulder. "I'm serious, kid. You don't want to mess with Emperor Bull. He's even bigger and stronger than Okra Joe. He carries a truncheon as long as a cane, and he gets real pleasure out of using it on rail riders."

"Truncheon?"

"A club. He's even named his, calls it Betty Sue. A

truncheon's usually made of wood, but Betty Sue is heavy iron, and he can swing her like she's a feather. He and Betty Sue have killed a lot of rail riders, Squatch. He would have no problem killing one as young as you."

Squatch put the can of spray paint into her hoodie pocket. "Guess I'll go home then."

"Home? So you ain't a rail kid after all."

"Nah, man. I just don't know which direction to go in this fog."

"I'll show you how to get out to the main road." Cabbage Patch led her through the fog to a line of freight cars. They walked along one, and he pointed ahead. "Follow this train 'til you get to the caboose, make a left, and after a couple dozen steps you'll come to railroad tracks. Cross the first set and follow the second set to the right."

They passed an open space between two cars, and Cabbage Patch rose in the air, dropping the stick with his bundle. He disappeared into the dark and fog. It happened so quickly that Squatch stood a second, not sure what she'd seen. Then came the sounds of a fight, grunts and scuffling. Squatch stepped between the freight cars and saw a huge man, bigger than Okra Joe, standing on the coupling that connected the cars. In one hand he held Cabbage Patch by his neck, and his other held a long club.

Squatch started forward to help Cabbage Patch.

With the big man's hand around his throat, Cabbage Patch forced out two words. "Run, Squatch."

Emperor Bull turned his eyes to her; they glowed like there was fire behind them, and she bolted from between the cars and ran blindly in the fog. There was a sound like a fist hitting a baseball glove really hard, and it repeated several more times. After covering some distance, she realized she'd made a mistake by running off in a panic. She should have turned left once she got out of that little space between the cars and followed the directions Cabbage Patch had given her. She turned completely around and hoped she was facing in the direction she'd come from to where Emperor Bull had taken Cabbage Patch. She had no desire to return there, but if she angled to the right, she'd still get back to the train, but farther along and closer to the exit. She walked slowly, trying to make as little noise as possible. The fog was helping, hiding her from Emperor Bull as well as muting any sound she made.

Squatch exhaled in relief when she got to a freight car. Turning right, she kept her left hand on it as she followed the directions Cabbage Patch had given. After what seemed like forever in the dark and fog, she got to the end of one car, and there was no other. She'd reached the end of the train.

"Hello, Squatch."

She jumped. Cabbage Patch perched on the top step of three stairs leading up onto the train car's deck. He sat in shadow, but she could still see his splintered skull, missing eye, and other wounds he'd suffered from the truncheon named Betty Sue.

"Emperor Bull got you, didn't he?"

"Oh, he did, kid. He got me like he's gotten me over and over and over ever since the first time he got me back in 1936."

"I don't understand."

Cabbage Patch patted the railing next to him. "This here's the caboose, Squatch. Get Emperor Bull to come back here."

"Why?"

Cabbage Patch winked his one remaining eye. "We will be waiting for him back here."

"I'm going home, Cabbage Patch. I just have to get to the second set of tracks and follow them to the main road."

Cabbage Patch looked sad. "I'm sorry, Squatch. It's too

late for you to get away. Your only chance is to lure him back to the caboose, where we will be waiting."

Squatch started to respond, but as she watched, Cabbage Patch faded until she was looking at the empty back deck of the car. She stood there a long time before finally finding the will to move. Before she took two steps, someone grabbed her by the back of her hoodie and lifted her up. Squatch was spun around until she found herself face-to-face with the man who'd taken the truncheon to Cabbage Patch. She was in the grasp of Emperor Bull.

Emperor Bull brought up his truncheon, Betty Sue. When he got a good look at Squatch, he stopped, and gave her a smile with teeth covered in green fuzz. Keeping his grip on her hoodie, he started toward the front of the train. She screamed, yelled, and struggled, but it didn't do any good. He got tired of it and shoved Squatch into the side of a freight car. It didn't knock her out, but it hurt, and she kept still the rest of the way. When they got to one car that had its door open, he flung her in like she didn't weigh any more than an empty backpack. Before she had a chance to shake it off, he climbed in after her and shoved her into a spindly ladder-back chair.

She sat before a flimsy wooden table, and he took a moment to use a match to light a lantern. He stood across the table and studied her. His head was blocky and shaved to a stubble. Whiskers darkened his chin and cheeks, and his nose was flat and twisted like a fighter's. His eyes were yellow and run through with spiderwebs of veins. On top of his head, he wore a blue police-style hat with a black brim. His wool jacket hung to mid-thigh and was crossed with a leather belt across his stomach, attached to another wide black belt that looped over one shoulder. A brass badge etched with RAILROAD SECURITY was pinned to his chest. Like his jacket, his pants matched the color of his hat, and black stripes ran down the side of each leg. A thick leather strap ran through the handle of his truncheon, and he used it to spin Betty Sue like a propeller.

Squatch looked past him and saw something in the corner of the car. She knew she should keep her mouth shut, but her brother had once told her that writers had to be brave because they sometimes had to climb way high, or had to run from the cops, or had to fight other taggers.

She tried to sound as unafraid as possible. "Is that yours?" She gave her head one nod in the direction of the corner.

Emperor Bull turned and scowled. He crossed to the corner and picked up the doll that lay there. It had straight brown hair and wore a bright blue dress with two red leather shoes. He carried it to the open door. He tossed up the doll and used his truncheon like a baseball bat to hit it from the train car. Squatch heard the porcelain crack with the impact.

Emperor Bull returned to the table. "You're a breather, ain't you, lassie?"

"Huh?"

"Alive."

Squatch lifted her eyes to his. "You can't do this."

He laughed, actually saying, "Ho, ho, ho," like an evil Santa Claus. Pulling out the chair across from her, he sat, looking like a grown-up trying to sit in a chair in a kindergarten class. "I can do whatever I want, lassie. You're in my yard, on my train." His breath smelled of rotten eggs and an animal that'd been squashed by a car and cooked in the sun for a couple of days.

"They're not yours; you just work for the people who own the trains."

The smile left his face. He slowly pushed the lantern to the side of the table and leaned down, putting his face in hers. "When I'm here, the yard is mine, the trains are mine, and like any rail rider here, dead or alive, you, too, are mine."

He leaned back, and that sick smile returned. In Squatch's neighborhood there was a man named Mr. Doyle, who ran a little neighborhood store. He was real friendly, liked talking to the kids, and always had a joke or two. He immigrated from Ireland twenty or so years ago, and Squatch loved his Irish accent. Emperor Bull spoke in a similarly thick accent, but where Mr. Doyle's voice made her feel good, Emperor Bull's was malignant and made her feel like she was one step away from dying.

"Those men I talked to. They said you kill rail riders."

"The men who hired me didn't care how I did my job as long as I got results. And there was no one better than me at keeping rail riders out of their yards and off their trains. Companies all across the country hired me if they had problems. I've worked in California, for a line in New Jersey, the Chicago yards, all the rails and yards in between. I was a specialist, you see, guaranteed their rail rider problems would end after a few weeks with me on the job."

"I'm not a rail rider," she said.

"Oh, is that right, now?" He chuckled with his *ho, ho, ho.* "I been chasing 'em for a long time. I can smell 'em."

He leaned toward her and sniffed. "And I can smell it on you." Sniff, sniff. "Though you smell better than most." He aimed his truncheon at her and poked her shoulder. "You're a rail rat, and I'm the exterminator."

She chose that moment to try to escape and ran for the door. Emperor Bull's hand shot out, grabbed her, and threw her back into the chair. They stared at each other, and a train whistle blasted so loudly she jumped.

Emperor Bull nodded toward the front of the train and said, "Coal car is the next up, after which the locomotive."

Coal? How long has it been since trains ran on coal? she thought. They lurched. The train jerked again and again, and then they were moving. "What's going on?" There was panic in her voice.

"You're taking your final train ride, lassie."

Squatch stared out the open door and could tell by how the fog swirled that the train was picking up speed. Though she was no expert on trains, she had an idea that the old coal-powered trains needed miles to get moving fast. Yet they were already racing along. The fog thinned, and she looked out on an unfamiliar landscape, illuminated by a full moon, the night stars, and the occasional light of a distant farmhouse. Squatch lived in a city; she should've been seeing the industrial area with all its warehouses and factories and manufacturing plants, not rolling hills and farmland. As the scenery flashed by, she knew they were going too fast for her to escape by jumping out of the train car.

She turned to Emperor Bull. "What now?"

He grinned and slowly stood, holding Betty Sue in one hand and slapping it down into the palm of the other. "In a hurry to meet your fate, eh, lassie?"

Squatch remembered what Cabbage Patch had said: *Your only chance is to lure him back to the caboose.* She was scared, terrified even, but if there was a chance, she'd take it.

"Yeah, you're a big man, huh? Going to beat a kid to death. How brave."

The smile dropped from Emperor Bull's face and turned into a snarl. He made a noise that was part growl and part snort. "This has been my job most of my life." His face shifted, growing dark in the lantern light. The shadows deepened under his cheekbones and eyes until he resembled a skull. "But I've been doing it a lot longer dead."

Squatch had already concluded she had somehow worked her way into a ghost story, and there was no denying that the ghost of Emperor Bull wanted to kill her.

She stared into his eyes.

His face returned to normal. "Perhaps you want to make a jump for it. Whether I kill you or you die falling from this train makes no matter; your soul will be mine."

She needed time to come up with an idea, so she kept him talking. "What do you mean, my soul will be yours?" She looked around the car like she was exploring her options.

He laughed and said, "Those I killed are buried in shallow graves, and because of the evil inflicted upon them, and because those graves are not hallowed, the ground they were buried in became profane."

With her back to the open door, she asked, "What happened to those you killed on trains?"

He gave her a wink. "I would stash their bodies back in the caboose until we stopped and I could dig another grave. Imagine my surprise when I was knocked from atop a freight car by a rail rider who went by the name of Indiana Pete. I died and refused to leave this world, because of which, the souls of all those I killed and buried in profane ground find themselves trapped between this world and the next, where I hunt and kill them again and again throughout all eternity." He gave a great sigh of satisfaction.

In her mind, she again heard Cabbage Patch say, *Your*

only chance is to lure him back to the caboose, where we will be waiting. Now she knew whom he meant by *we*.

"This isn't a real train, is it?" she asked.

"It's as real as it gets for you. But of all the trains I've ridden over the years, this was the one waiting for me. An amalgamation of all the trains upon which I worked. You're riding a ghost train. You're as good as a ghost yourself."

Squatch was at the door, the wind whipping at her clothes. The door swung to the right toward the coal car. Next to it was an iron ladder attached to the side of the freight car, leading up to the roof. She definitely didn't want to get out there and climb it, but there was no choice. She still had the can of spray paint in her hoodie pocket. She took a deep breath, pulled it out, and, shaking it, walked up to Emperor Bull.

"I got something for you." Squatch sprayed a thick line of Montana Brand Vivid Red across his eyes.

He roared and swung Betty Sue blindly. Squatch ducked under the truncheon, feeling the breeze it made as it whooshed over her head. She rushed to the door and placed one of the chairs next to the opening. Stepping on it, she reached out to grab hold of the top of the door. Rather than hang from it with her arms extended fully, she did half a pull-up so her arms were bent ninety degrees. She slid her left hand along the door and then slid her right hand after her, left, right, left, right. Because of the train's high speed, her clothes and legs were blowing around like she was in a hurricane. She kept her grip and moved closer to the ladder. Despite the deafening winds, she still could hear Emperor Bull flailing about with his truncheon. She got to the metal ladder, which was a foot from the end of the door. Not a long distance, but she was on a speeding train, feeling every bounce, the wind trying to pull her free, and all the while hanging by her hands from the top of a railcar door. She slid her right hand next to her face, and then she reached out with her left and grasped a rung. Next, she swung out her left foot, which slid off the ladder. That simple act nearly had her falling to her death. She gripped harder, tried again, and put her foot on a rung. From there she moved fully onto the ladder.

Squatch scurried up onto the roof of the freight car. As fast as they traveled, and as bouncy as the ride was, she spread her feet wide and lowered her body for better balance in the extreme winds. Though the roofs of these train cars angled down slightly, the center length of each had a two-foot-wide deck to give rail workers some stability when working up high. She turned to the front of the train, past the coal car to the locomotive. Thick smoke, as black as tar, erupted from the smokestack, rising overhead and trailing into the night. Turning the other way, she groaned at the length of the train.

Proceeding carefully, she made it to the end of the first car. There was a four-foot space between it and the next, with two hook-shaped couplers joined together like the fingers of two people preparing to thumb wrestle. A metal ladder was attached at each end of the cars. After a quick glance to make sure Emperor Bull wasn't coming, she made her way carefully down the ladder. At the bottom, she studied the couplers holding the cars together. She figured she could take one big step out to where they locked together, giving her the biggest area on which to plant her foot, and then another step to get her other foot onto the other ladder. One misstep, and she'd fall and get chopped into pieces by steel wheels. Squatch made her move and found herself safely gripping the other ladder. She climbed up on top of the next freight car and repeated the procedure several times until she was on top of the ninth car.

Glancing back, Squatch saw Emperor Bull on top of the car they'd been in. A dark figure silhouetted by darker smoke from the smokestack, and with a thick line of red paint across his face, he looked demonic. He started running. As big as he was, he was fast and graceful. He didn't slow a bit when he got to the end of the car, launching himself through the air and landing on the roof of the next. Without stopping, he ran and leaped again to the next car.

Adrenaline flushed through Squatch's body. She turned and ran. Figuring if he could do it, she could, too, she jumped at the end of the freight car. She landed on the next, but lost her balance, and stumbled. She dropped to her knees and stopped sliding a few inches from the edge. No longer looking back, she was up and running. After several cars, she got into a rhythm of running and jumping.

As fast as she was going, Emperor Bull was faster. His breathing, like a snorting boar, was closer. Squatch made another jump, and when she had her feet securely on the deck of the freight car roof, she chanced a quick look back. Screaming, she threw herself flat, and a second later the ghost train shot into a tunnel. There was less than three feet from the top of the train to the tunnel ceiling. Had she not looked back, she would have been another soul in Emperor Bull's collection.

His legs stood on the car behind hers. Only visible from the knees down, they stood stock-still. Where his legs touched the ceiling of the tunnel, there was a glow that shimmered and flickered. She rationalized that since he was a ghost, he could pass through solid objects, and that's what the rest of his body was doing, passing through the mountain they were riding through.

She crawled to the end of the car, went down the ladder, made it to the ladder of the next car and went up. In that fashion she gained a lead of a half dozen freight cars by the time the train exited the tunnel. Once out, their train-top race started again. Squatch lost track of how many cars she'd jumped; it seemed to go on forever. Caught in the rhythm of running and jumping, she leaped from one car to the next, continuing to run until she saw that there was no car after it. She stopped and stumbled to the very edge of the caboose's roof, her arms windmilling as she got her balance. She cast a hasty glance back. Emperor Bull was still coming, and they were separated by only a few cars. Climbing off the roof and onto the ladder, Squatch descended to the rear deck, opened the door, and stepped into darkness. With hands held out, she slowly made her way into the caboose. She bumped into a chair and then a table.

A third of the way in, she felt buzzing along her flesh, recognizing it as a growing energy like static electricity. There was a sound, a murmur that was hard to discern over the clickety-clack of the hurtling train. Voices, she realized, countless voices talking at once. Their volume increased, and she stood still to try to understand what was being said.

He's on his way.

He comes.

Emperor Bull is coming.

"Cabbage Patch?" Squatch whispered. She felt his hand, as subtle as a feather on her shoulder.

You're a brave rail rider, Squatch. Bravest I've ever known. Your job is almost done, but you're still not safe. Get yourself to the back of the caboose and lure him in when he comes. And stay out of reach of Betty Sue.

The voices were louder now. So many were talking at once she couldn't make out specific words, just the tone of what was being said. And what she heard was getting angrier and angrier.

She started for the back, bumping into what she thought was another table, but after feeling it, she realized it was a bar. She walked its length and continued until she reached the rear wall. She turned and put her back to it just as the open door darkened with Emperor Bull's arrival.

"A good chase, but not good enough." He had to bend down to fit his bulk through the caboose door. "Where are ya, lassie?"

Squatch tried to speak, but she was so terrified that nothing came out. Her hands trembled, and she placed them flat against the wall. She cleared her voice and spoke loudly. "Come get me, if you got the guts." She tried to put defiance into her voice, but to her ears, she sounded like a frightened girl.

"Ho, ho, ho! If I got the guts. That's rich." A clang rang out as he swung Betty Sue into something metallic. Another clang followed that, and then a thump and a crack as he hit and broke something wooden. "Hear that, lassie? That'll be your head."

She pressed into the wall, wishing she could back up farther.

Crash!

He got closer.

Clang!

And closer.

She heard Betty Sue cleave the air, and the truncheon

passed an inch from her head. One more swing, she knew, and she'd ride the train forever.

"Hello, Emperor Bull." It was Cabbage Patch's voice. Dozens more voices echoed it.

Emperor Bull.

Emperor Bull.

Emperor Bull.

"Who's there?" Emperor Bull demanded.

We are.

We are.

We are.

The lives you took.

The souls you stole.

We've been waiting for you.

Here in the caboose.

In the caboose.

...the caboose.

...caboose.

There was no light source, yet a glow filled the room so that Squatch could see as if a single candle had been lit. The caboose was filled with people. Had they been flesh and blood, there's no way they could have all fit. But they overlapped, held the same spaces, and encircled Emperor Bull. His face reflected a terror that all his victims must have shown in their last moments. He pulled back his arm and swung Betty Sue. Over and over, he lashed out at those around him, but his truncheon passed through their bodies. He stopped and looked at Betty Sue as if it were defective. When he brought his gaze back up, all the souls swept over him so that he was no longer visible. He shouted with a combination of rage and terror, and every few seconds his arm emerged from the mass of ghosts, swinging Betty Sue.

The throng shifted closer to the bar, and Squatch saw a chance to escape. She ran past the horde, ducking as Betty Sue swung over her head. Emperor Bull screamed shrilly, and the shift to silence was so abrupt that the myriad voices echoed in her head. She ran out the door, and even though the train was still traveling fast, she jumped from the deck of the caboose.

As her feet left the train, time stopped, and she hung in the air. Faint voices came to her from the open door. Those she could understand were thanking her for what she had done. Thanking her for freeing them.

Cabbage Patch's voice was the clearest. *Thank you, Squatch. Now we'll all make it to the Big Rock Candy Mountain.*

Somehow, she instinctively knew it was the rail rider term for paradise—for heaven.

Time started back up, and she barely had the chance to scream before she fell.

Squatch blinked and gazed up. She was at the train yard, lying on her back, staring up at the railcar she'd planned to paint and the ladder she was going to use leaning against it.

Shaky, she got to her feet. She pulled the can of Montana Brand Vivid Red from her hoodie pocket. She ascended the ladder and spray-painted *Cabbage Patch* on the railcar in letters so big that she had to move the ladder three times to get it done. Then Squatch picked up her paints and her father's ladder and started for home.

- CHAPTER 10 -

THE GREAT WHITE NOTHING

Tristan walked into the room with a half-empty pizza box. "Where's Gabby? When the power comes back on, her wizard has to say the incantation."

Noelle, a redhead in jeans and a T-shirt, said, "She went out on the porch to see if the power outage hit the entire neighborhood or if it's just us."

Tristan put the pizza box on a coffee table and strode down the hallway to the open front door. Pushing on the screen, he stepped out. Gabby stood at the top of the porch steps.

"Is it a neighborhood outage or just..." Tristan looked out and blinked several times in confusion. "What—the—heck?"

"Yeah." Gabby stood with her hands on the porch railing. She colored her blond hair with tinges of blue. She was fun to hang with, most everyone thought she was cool, and she had an off-the-charts IQ.

"What is—where is—well—everything?"

Gabby shook her head and shrugged.

Where Tristan's lawn ended, there was only white. Past the end of the driveway, there was white. Where the other houses, streets, trees, and horizon should be was blank white space. And the sky? It was gone as well and replaced with white.

"You see it, too, right?" Gabby asked. "Or maybe the right way to phrase it is, you don't see it, don't see anything past your lawn, do you?"

It was Tristan's birthday, and he expected surprises, but nothing like this. He was the ripe old age of fourteen. His parents had been all gung-ho to throw him a birthday party, and on one hand, he liked the idea. On the other, he was worried it would seem babyish. So he compromised by having his best friend, Gordie, come over, along with Noelle and her best friend, Gabby. Tristan was doing this for Gordie as well, seeing as he'd had a crush on Noelle for a long time. Tristan let his folks call it a party and didn't protest when his mom hung up decorations.

For his birthday, he had gotten a new video game, *Thieves of Infinity*, and they planned a day of playing it while stuffing themselves with pizza, cake, and soda. His parents said he was old enough for responsibility and trust, so they left the kids alone while they went to a matinee movie.

Tristan and Gabby heard the screen door open and close, but neither turned around.

Gordie came out. He was shorter than Tristan, his dark hair was clipped close, and he wore thick, round glasses. In a tentative voice, he asked, "Guys, what's going on?"

Noelle stepped up as well and could only say, "What?"

"Gabby?" Tristan said.

"I don't know. It's bizarre."

Noelle's face turned red. She put a finger in Tristan's face and moved it back and forth from him to Gordie. "Is this a joke? Something you guys think is funny?"

"What? No!" Gordie said.

"Really, Noelle. We don't know what's happening any more than you," Tristan said, and leaned out over the porch railing to try to see farther.

Gabby backed up a step and dropped into the porch swing.

After a couple of minutes of silent staring, Gordie sat

next to her. "Gabby, you're the smartest kid in school. You gotta have some idea."

"I don't. I mean, if I had to guess, I'd say it started when the power went out."

They'd just gotten to the third level of *Thieves of Infinity*, and Noelle, who was the warrior, Ragor the Rager, was facing off against the one-horned cyclops. The picture on the flat screen scrambled, lights flared brighter, and there was a loud hum of electricity, followed by a crackling noise. A second later the power went out.

Gabby pulled her cell phone from a pocket and started hitting buttons. "I'll see if the power's out at my house, too." She put the phone to her ear. After twenty seconds, she lowered it. "Nothing."

"See if you can find anything about what's happening on the internet," Gordie said.

Gabby nodded and fiddled with her cell some more. "No Wi-Fi, no data."

"Be right back," Tristan said, and rushed into the house. He emerged a minute later. "Our landline is dead, too. No dial tone."

Gordie got up from the swing, moved to the porch steps, and took a tentative step down.

"Are you sure you want to do that?" Tristan asked.

Gordie ignored him and slowly descended the final three and stood on the sidewalk that led to the driveway. Tristan joined him a second later, followed by Gabby.

Noelle stayed on the porch. "Be careful, you guys."

Gabby stepped onto the grass and took a moment before bringing out her other foot. She stood there and then gave a little hop up and down. She started, step by slow step, to walk to the lawn's end.

"I'm not so sure that's smart," Tristan said, but then followed. Gordie trailed behind him.

"Really, guys, be careful." Noelle sounded near tears.

Gabby turned back to her. "I think it's something we have to do, I mean, if we want to figure out what's going on."

Tristan picked up a dead branch from under an oak tree. Gabby stopped a foot from where the grass ended and the nothingness began. Gordie and Tristan moved next to her.

"I'm not staying up here by myself," Noelle shouted, and came off the porch to join them.

Gabby and Tristan exchanged wide-eyed glances, and then Tristan moved even closer to the whiteness.

"Oh man," Noelle muttered, a tremble in her voice.

Tristan extended the branch, which was between two

and three feet long, out over the border of where the grass met the white nothing.

"Ho-lee cow," Gabby said.

The part of the branch that passed just over the border went out of focus. Tristan pushed it out farther, and the tip broke apart into dozens, if not hundreds, of tiny pieces.

"The pieces, they're little squares," Gordie said.

"Yes, they are," Gabby said. "Hmmm."

When Tristan pushed the stick out even farther, the tip vanished completely.

"Interesting," Gabby said. "Pull it back."

He did, and where it had broken into little squares, the pieces re-formed into the branch, but it was shorter than before, because where it vanished did not come back.

Noelle gasped and pointed to where the driveway ended. "Look." Half the mailbox that faced the street had broken into those little square pieces.

Gabby ran over and then pointed at the ground. "It's not only the mailbox. The end of the driveway and the lawn are breaking up. I think the great white nothing is closing in."

"Great white nothing?" Gordie said.

"I think it fits," Gabby said.

"Ooooh." Gordie's face had turned pale. "I don't feel so good."

"Why don't you go sit down?" Noelle said, and took his elbow, guiding him to the porch. Gordie dropped onto the steps, and Noelle sat next to him. "If you're dizzy, put your head between your knees."

Head down, Gordie said, "Just give me a minute, I'll be okay."

Tristan watched Noelle and Gordie a moment, then leaned close to Gabby and whispered, "You figured something out, didn't you?"

Gabby tapped a finger against her chin. "Maybe, but I want to be sure before I say anything. Is your drone still working?"

"Yeah, why?"

"Go get it."

Gabby returned to the porch while Tristan ran into the house. A couple of minutes later he came out with both hands grasping an orange drone with black trim and its controller. Four arms extended from the center of the drone, and at the end of each was a black propeller.

"Put it out there," Gabby told him.

Tristan passed the drone controller to Gabby, then ran down the steps and placed the drone on the lawn.

Gabby fiddled with the controls, and the propellers began to spin. Tristan ran back up onto the porch and took the controller.

"Where to?" Tristan asked.

Gabby pointed straight up. "About twenty feet."

Noelle and Gordie stood as the drone lifted a foot, rocked back and forth a couple of times, and then shot straight up.

"Not too fast," Gabby warned.

"Okay." Tristan stepped out from the porch and looked up. "Twenty feet."

The others came down to join him.

"Fly around your yard, but don't go into the great white nothing. Do you have any binoculars?"

"Yeah. Gordie, can you run and get them?" Tristan said.

"On it." Gordie rushed into the house.

After Tristan made a circuit of his yard, Gordie came charging out the front door holding up a pair of binoculars. He passed them to Gabby.

Tristan hovered the drone directly overhead.

Gabby focused on it with the binoculars. "Okay, really slow. Take it higher." After it had gone up ten more feet, she said, "Stop." The drone hovered in place. "Take it up a foot. Another foot. Another."

They repeated this several more times, and then the drone lurched and fell.

"What the—" Tristan's thumbs worked at levers and switches as the drone plummeted a dozen feet, then stopped and maintained altitude.

"What happened?" Noelle asked.

Gabby brought down the binoculars and said, "What I expected. The propellers pixelated, and the drone dropped until they re-formed."

"Pixelated?" Gordie asked.

Gabby squatted. "Remember what happened when Tristan stuck the branch out past the lawn?"

"Yeah, it broke into little pieces."

"Little square pieces, like pixels." Gabby picked at the grass and stared out into the white nothing. "You know what pixels are, right?"

Noelle said, "The little squares that make up pictures on a computer."

"Yeah, digital images are really hundreds of thousands or even millions of pixels that join together to make up an image. When you break those images down into little squares, you're pixelating them. I was watching for that through these." Gabby held up the binoculars. "When it reached a certain height, the propellers pixelated, and

the drone fell until they re-formed and the drone could fly again." She put the binoculars on one of the porch steps.

"Meaning?" Gordie said.

"If Tristan had flown the drone up at full speed, the propellers would have reached a higher altitude and not only pixelated, but vanished. The propellers would not have reformed, and the drone would have crashed."

Tristan brought the drone down and landed it softly on the lawn. "What are you getting at, Gabby?"

"The great white nothing is not only closing in from around us, but from above as well."

"Oh no, look." Noelle pointed at the end of the driveway. The great white nothing was creeping closer, and all that was left of the mailbox were a few black pixels.

Gabby ran for the house. "Come on, everybody, I want to check out Tristan's basement."

They hurried through the front door and down the hallway to the kitchen. Tristan paused to reach into the pantry for a flashlight.

"Don't think you'll need it," Gabby said.

"Power's out; no lights down there." Tristan switched on the flashlight.

Gabby gave him a sad smile. "You'll see."

Tristan led them three-quarters of the way down the wooden steps into the basement. The basement floor was breaking up into pixels, white showing between the tiny squares.

"The great white nothing is closing in from below, too," Tristan said.

Noelle pinched Gabby's ear and forced her to look at her. "Gabby, I can tell you know something. Tell us what's going on."

"Ouch, okay. Let's go into the kitchen and have a seat first."

They went up and sat around the kitchen table. Tristan got everybody a soda.

Gabby took a long drink and said, "There are some people, Elon Musk among them, who have questioned whether our reality is really just a computer simulation."

"What?" Noelle said.

Gordie and Tristan exchanged a glance.

"They wonder if we're really part of a computer program or a computer game, something like that."

"That's stupid," Gordie protested. "Why would anyone want to play a computer game with us? Compared with *Thieves of Infinity*, our reality is pretty dull."

"To us, maybe," Gabby said. "But if you could ask the

characters in *Thieves of Infinity*, they might say their lives were pretty boring."

"So you're saying somebody is playing a computer game and we're the characters?" Tristan asked.

"It's a theory."

"It's stupid," Gordie muttered.

Gabby shrugged. "Look at games like *The Sims* and all the other life-simulation games."

"*Animal Crossing*," Tristan said.

"*BitLife*," Noelle said.

"Right. How do we know that those characters don't think they're really alive, that to them, their reality is—well—real."

"It's stupid," Gordie said for the third time, but he didn't sound as sure of himself. "If that's the case, then what's with the great white nothing?"

"Maybe they're shutting down the game." Gabby thought a moment. "But no, if that were the case, we probably wouldn't know it, we'd just pick up where we left off when they start up the game again."

Noelle slowly brought up her gaze, her face reflecting fear. "Maybe a computer virus?"

Gabby nodded. "Could be. My guess, however, is the game is crashing."

"So there's nothing we can do," Tristan said in a resigned tone. "We're just going to pixelate into nothing."

"Will it hurt?" Noelle asked in a hushed tone.

Gabby didn't answer, and no one spoke.

A few moments later Gabby jumped from her chair, ran to the kitchen window, and looked out. The great white nothing had advanced over half the lawn toward the house. "There's still time, come on."

They followed Gabby out the side door into the garage. It was fairly neat, with tools attached to the walls, a freezer in a corner, and lots of items set up high on shelves.

"Any house paint in here?" Gabby asked.

Tristan ran over to a cabinet and opened a door, then another, and started pulling out random items and throwing them over his shoulder: a bunched-up canvas drop cloth, a tangled orange extension cord, and a dirty doll with a blue dress and cracked face. "Aha." He pulled out two half-full gallon paint cans and handed one to Gordie and kept the other.

"Shake them up," Gabby said. She poked around the cabinet, retrieving four large paintbrushes. "Here." She handed those to Noelle, then grabbed a screwdriver and stuck it in her back pocket.

"What have you got planned?" Tristan asked.

"She's not making any sense," Gordie said.

"Just do what I say," Gabby shouted. "Noelle, over here, please help me with the ladder."

Noelle looked at the aluminum ladder mounted on the wall and stuck the paintbrushes into her pockets. Gabby got one end of the ladder, and Noelle took the other.

"Open the garage door," Gabby ordered.

Tristan twisted a handle on the garage door and pulled it up, giving them room to get out.

"Hurry," Gabby said. They rushed outside, Gordie and Tristan shaking the paint cans. With Noelle's help, Gabby extended the ladder to its full height and leaned it against the house. "Get climbing, guys."

Noelle went first, rushing up. Gabby followed, and then Gordie and Tristan, both of whom climbed slower because they carried the paint cans. After Gordie got on the roof, he put his can down and took Tristan's. Tristan started onto the roof, but the ladder fell to the side, and he yelped, thinking he was going with it. But he managed to grab the roof with both hands, while he hooked the roof's edge with the heel of his left foot. Gordie, Noelle, and Gabby hurried to the edge, each grabbing a part of him and pulling him up.

"Whew! Thanks. Thought I was a goner."

Looking over the side, they saw that the great white nothing had reached where they'd planted the bottom of the ladder. It had pixelated and fallen.

"The great white nothing is closing in faster." Gordie's voice shook.

"Pay attention!" Gabby shouted. She grabbed the brushes from Noelle's pockets and passed them around, then she used the screwdriver to open the paint cans and tossed the lids over the side of the roof. She handed a can of white to Tristan and kept a can of yellow. With her free hand, she pointed to the black shingles on the roof. "Noelle, you start right there. Paint the letter *R*, make sure it's big, five feet tall. Tristan, print a big *E* next to it. Gordie, next to Tristan's *E*, paint a *B* just as big, and I'll do the next letter."

"I don't understand," Noelle shouted, even though she'd already dipped her paintbrush into the can Tristan held and started on her letter.

"You'll see," Gabby said.

When Noelle finished her five-foot *R*, Gabby assigned her another letter next to the one she was working on, and then she told Tristan to print the last letter. When Gabby was done with her letter, she went to the end of the word and added an exclamation point.

They stood back and looked at the sloppily written word, *REBOOT!*

The edge of the roof was pixelating.

Gabby looked up into the sky and started shouting, "Hey! Hey out there! Help!"

They looked at her a moment before joining in, screaming for help, waving and gesturing at the sky. Noelle shrieked as loudly as she could. Their yells and screams got louder and more frenzied as more of the roof vanished and the pixelating closed in.

"Reboot! Reboot!"

"Help us! Reboot!"

"Hey you, out there!"

The circle of existence got smaller and smaller, and they had to stand closer and closer.

Gabby stopped shouting and told Noelle, "It doesn't hurt." She pointed down, and everyone looked at her feet. The front of her shoes had broken into pixels.

The great white nothing shrunk their space more, and all their feet were pixelating.

"Tristan, duck!" Gabby yelled.

The top of his head was breaking into tiny squares.

And then, everything went black.

After the great white nothing, the instant shift to black was startling.

Noelle screamed, which caused Gordie to scream.

"Guys?" Tristan said.

"I'm here."

"Me too."

"Me too."

"What's happening?" Noelle asked. "Are we dead?"

"Just wait," Gabby said over and over in an anticipating tone, and then shouted, "Brace yourselves."

A second later it was like someone hit a light switch and they could see. The abrupt change caused Noelle to lose her balance on the steep roof, and she stumbled toward the edge. Gordie caught her by her wrist, and she righted herself. The roof was back under their feet, as was the house. They could see some of the lawn from their perspective.

"Look, the street," Gordie said like it was one of the world's wonders.

"And all the houses," Noelle said.

"And the trees," Tristan piped up.

"Look at the neighborhood," Gabby added.

One by one they ascended to the peak of the roof and

sat down, looking out over the *REBOOT!* they had painted on the rooftop to the surrounding neighborhood.

"I'm not sure I can get used to the idea that we're just part of a computer game," Noelle said.

Gordie nodded. "Yeah, but I'm glad everything is back to normal."

"What if it happens again?" Tristan asked.

"I don't know." Gabby shrugged. "What I'm really wondering is how you're going to explain to your dad about the giant *REBOOT!* we painted on the roof."

They all laughed, and then one by one they stopped and looked up.

Gabby got to her feet, pointed to the sky, and yelled, "Hey! Thanks for rebooting."

– CHAPTER 11 –

FOLLOW THE READER

Independence. Freedom. The ability to go where you want, when you want, to do whatever you want. This would be the summer of his independence. He was thirteen now, a teenager, and he figured he was due more freedom based on that. His friends called him DJ, and he was a normal everyday kind of guy. He was just starting to grow tall, with thick brown hair and blue eyes. One thing that set him apart was his obsession with games that he invented.

His mom was a nurse, and at the beginning of summer was switched to work the second shift. She was at the hospital from four until midnight five nights a week, which left him with all the freedom a kid could want during the summer.

His mom had asked a couple of neighbors to keep an eye on him, but he could sneak away pretty easily by going out the back door and through the woods behind his house. She wanted the neighbors to watch out for him mainly because of a psychopath called Popper. Kids had started vanishing from different parts of the state a few months earlier. Eight were currently missing. At first, police thought they were running away, which then inspired other kids to do the same. But that was before a girl who'd disappeared in the next town over had returned with her tale of Popper. Just before school let out for the summer, she left a drama rehearsal and was abducted. Popper took her to a dilapidated old cabin out in the country, blindfolded her, and used handcuffs to secure her to a chair. He then, with great delight, read her stories and poems by Edgar Allan Poe. He told her that when he was done reading to her, the real fun would begin.

She had something unique about one of her hands. She could dislocate her left thumb at will. She did that as he recited "The Raven," allowing her to slide the handcuffs off that wrist. The man was looking down at his book of Poe and didn't notice her remove the blindfold. She rushed to the fireplace and picked up a piece of firewood. He chased her, and she hit him with the wood, stunning him. She ran off, handcuffs still locked around one wrist, got to the road, and flagged down a car. By the time she returned with the police, the man had abandoned the little cabin and left no clues as to his identity.

She couldn't provide much of a description; she'd been terrified and could only remember that he was of medium size, had brown hair with a cowlick, and had a long, straight nose. The one thing that really stood out was that when the man had read from the book of Poe, he'd stutter whenever he came across the letter *p*, making a popping sound. "Once up-puh-puh-puh-pon a midnight dreary, while I puh-puh-puh-pondered, weak and weary..." Thus, he was christened Popper.

When DJ's mom checked on him, she called or texted his cell phone. They did have a landline in the house, but neither of them used it much. He'd tell her he was home, even though he might be a couple of miles away. And usually when that happened, he was with his friends and playing one of his games.

DJ designed those games, the kind you play outdoors. The first one he came up with was the previous summer. It was a combination of football, basketball, and baseball that he christened *Allball*.

As time passed, his games started getting more elaborate. They used an old, abandoned industrial park for *Zombie Infestation*, they played *Mermania* at the lake, and *Dodge, Duck, and Destroy* could be played anywhere as long as you had a ball, three balloons, and a musical instrument.

DJ called his latest game *Follow the Reader*. Games started at any of the library branches or bookstores. They played with two-person teams. Each would select a stranger for the other team to follow, what they called *the mark*. The team that followed their mark the longest was the winner. If a team followed the mark for a full hour without being noticed, that'd also be a win. Well, almost. At the end of the hour, the followers had to use a cell phone to take a picture of the mark, complete with a time stamp. Most losses happened when a mark got in a car and drove off. Another way a team could lose was if the mark noticed they were being followed.

DJ was with three friends, Eddie, Ronnie, and Derek. They were hanging out in front of the downtown branch of the library just after dusk, ready to kick off a round of *Follow the Reader*. Ronnie was short and a little heavy; Derek was tall and thin with blazing red hair. Eddie was DJ's best friend, and Eddie was a girl. Her real name was Edwina, which, everyone agreed, was even worse than DJ's first name, which was why he went by his initials. Eddie and DJ had been good friends since the first grade, but he'd recently started to look at her differently. He thought she was really pretty. Sometimes he'd find himself staring at her with strange sensations in his chest, and if she caught him looking at her, she smiled in a way that made his face heat up. Because of her long, silky blond hair, she wore a hoodie to play *Follow the Reader*; it made her less noticeable.

"Ronnie and I won the last game," Derek said.

"Bull," Eddie said. "That was the guy and his daughter from the mall."

"Yeah, but we got twenty minutes in before he noticed us."

Ronnie added, "Thought we were stalking his daughter or something and chased us off."

"And we followed our mark for twenty-two minutes before she caught an Uber," Eddie said.

"Oh yeah," Derek said.

"Oh yeah," Eddie echoed in a mocking tone.

DJ told them, "Doesn't matter. Tonight's a new round."

"DJ and me against you two," Eddie said. DJ played it cool even though he loved that he and Eddie were always on the same team.

"All right, let's pick our marks," Derek said, crossing his arms and leaning back against the marble lion statue in front of the library.

Eddie put a hand on DJ's arm. "We got this." He warmed at the contact.

Sitting against the base of the lion statue, they watched people going and coming from the stone building. A woman in her forties came out of the library, retrieved a phone from her purse, and called someone. DJ and Eddie exchanged a glance.

"Her," Eddie said, pointing out Ronnie and Derek's mark.

A guy came out of the library with a big book in his hand. Ronnie and Derek whispered to each other, then Ronnie nodded in the man's direction. "Him."

In his thirties, he was kind of nerdy-looking. The man paused and tucked the book under his left arm. He pulled a comb from a pocket and ran it through his brown hair, combing it straight back. He wore a brown sport coat over a white button-down shirt. He slipped the comb back into the pocket of his matching slacks and started walking again, passing right in front of them. They got up to follow, and Eddie pulled the hoodie over her head.

"We'll meet you guys in a little over an hour." DJ checked the time on his cell phone. "It's nine thirteen."

"Happy following," Derek said. He and Ronnie were resting against the stone lion since the woman was still on the phone.

DJ silenced his phone, then he and Eddie started down the stone steps after their mark. While his phone was still in his hand, it vibrated. He checked caller ID. "Be quiet," he told Eddie. "It's Mom." He pressed the Talk icon and said, "Hey, Mom."

"Hi, Dexter," she said. That's what the *D* in DJ stood for. The *J* was for *James*. DJ didn't mind the *James*, but he hated the *Dexter*. She asked, "What are you up to?"

"Ah, not much." Right then a car down the street honked its horn.

"What's that? Where are you?"

"Sorry, watching TV. Let me turn it down," DJ said, hoping the car's driver wouldn't honk again.

"Well, stay in and lock the doors. I was just calling to check on you."

"Okay. See ya." He quickly ended the call.

Eddie looked at him with a serious expression, which made her even more striking. "Doesn't it bother you to lie to your mom like that?"

"No," DJ said, noting his defensive tone. "Besides, what'd you tell your mom?"

"I told her we were going to the library. Which is true— in a way."

DJ wished he'd thought of that. Though he said that lying to his mom didn't bother him, in reality it did. A lot. He shrugged off the guilt, and they continued after the mark. So far, he was keeping to the sidewalks of down-town. He stopped a few times to look in shop windows, but he never turned back to see them.

He went into the frozen yogurt place on Main Street, and DJ checked the time. "Forty-four minutes to go."

"If he doesn't get into a car before then," Eddie added.

"He won't. Think positive." DJ looked around.

"Should we split up?" Eddie asked.

DJ nodded. "That'll be safer. You go across the street and down to the next corner and wait. I'll hang out here on this side of the street. If he comes out and goes your way, you take the lead and I'll follow you. If he comes back this way, I'll take the lead and you follow me."

"Okay." She trotted across the street, stopped a moment when she got across from the frozen yogurt store to look in, then continued down to the corner.

Trying to look casual, DJ leaned against the wall of a building. Ten minutes later the mark came out, wiping his lips with a paper napkin. He stuffed it into a pocket and once again pulled out his comb and ran it from front to back across his head. DJ glanced down and picked at his fingernails while keeping the mark in his peripheral vision. The mark looked toward him for a second, then turned and walked the other way. Eddie sat at the curb, under a streetlight, and watched the mark. DJ thought she was too obvious, but the mark didn't seem to notice her.

When the mark got to the corner, Eddie got up and followed him from her side of the street. As DJ walked, he focused more on Eddie, on how graceful she was as she maneuvered through the pedestrians and up the sidewalk. The mark, meanwhile, meandered like he had nowhere to be, just out enjoying the night. Time passed as the game progressed, and soon they were down to only sixteen minutes left. The mark stopped in front of Bronski's Bookstore. It was closed at this time of night, and dark inside. Still, he peered into storefront windows that angled in on each side of the door so that the door was set farther back from the sidewalk. Eddie walked past the mark and continued on about ten yards before she stopped and sat at the curb. DJ stopped ten yards from Bronski's, leaned against a mailbox, and pretended he was texting.

While DJ had his phone out, he figured he'd go ahead and get a few preliminary pictures of the mark. He switched on the phone's photo function. The mark was gazing in the window that angled from the right of the door out to the sidewalk when DJ took the first photo. Then he took another one when the mark moved to look in the window to the left of the door. A minute later the mark combed his hair into place. With his library book tucked under his left arm, he continued up the street. A minute later DJ and Eddie resumed their places, the mark in front, Eddie a little back and across the street, and DJ farther back on the mark's side of the street.

When DJ got to Bronski's, he stopped and looked in the

windows. Other than the books right against the window, the store was too dark to see into. In fact, because of the window's reflection, he could see more of what was on the street than inside. Looking at the window to the left of the door, DJ could see the curb where Eddie sat while the mark window-shopped. DJ went to the right-side window and checked that reflection, seeing the mailbox he'd leaned against. The little hairs on his arms stood up. He made a mental note to tell the guys to be careful of reflections in windows when playing *Follow the Reader*.

At the outskirts of the busy downtown area, the mark crossed to Eddie's side of the street and went through the gate of the historical cemetery. It contained three dozen graves that dated back to the late eighteen hundreds. It was also a small park, with benches and markers. DJ checked the time and grinned, seeing they had only three minutes and one photo of the mark until they could proclaim themselves the winners.

DJ texted Derek, How's your follow going?

A minute later Derek texted back, The lady noticed Ronnie was following her and started yelling at him. We had to bail.

Grinning, DJ texted Eddie, Hey, we've already won. Let's pack it in.

Thirty seconds later his phone buzzed. Eddie texted back, Mind if I get the pic anyway?

The honor is all yours, he told her.

Eddie got to the gate to the cemetery and peeked inside. A second later she slipped in. DJ sat at the curb almost directly across the street. While waiting for Eddie's triumphant return, he pulled up the two earlier photos he'd taken of the mark. The first was from when the mark was looking in the right-side window of Bronski's. DJ zoomed in to study the picture better and then saw why the mark used his comb so much. A stiff clump of hair had popped up at the crown of his head. DJ shifted to the second photo, where the mark stepped to the left-side window and DJ could see the library book under the mark's arm. DJ's fingers played over the cell phone screen, enlarging the picture. The title of the book was *Tales of Mystery and Imagination* by Edgar Allan Poe. Sudden chills ran up his spine. The girl who had escaped from Popper said he read Poe out loud to her. And then DJ remembered that in her scant description of the man, she said he had a cowlick. She also said he had a long, straight nose, which also fit with the mark.

Dazed, DJ slowly stood. He moved a few feet up the

street so that he could see directly into the historic cemetery park. Darkness was all that was visible, like when he passed Bronski's Bookstore and looked in the window. And then he remembered the reflections of Bronski's windows where both he and Eddie had been observing the mark. The mark *had* seen them and knew they were tailing him. And the mark was Popper. For a second DJ almost threw up. A second later he almost panicked and ran, but then he thought of Eddie.

Get out! He's on to us! he texted her.

He waited for Eddie to emerge from the cemetery gate, but there was no movement in the darkness across the street.

"Come on, Eddie. Come on." He texted her again, Get out of there, he's Popper!!!

At first, time moved slowly, but then it jumped ahead, and when he checked his phone, DJ saw that Eddie had been in the cemetery park for almost ten minutes. "I just need to get Eddie, that's all. Get her and get out," he muttered. Taking a breath, he ran across the street and entered the cemetery park.

It was small, not much more than an acre ringed by tall oak trees whose limbs blocked most of the surrounding light. What light did push through was filtered by thick strands of Spanish moss, giving it even more of a creepy vibe. DJ stuck to the right side, hoping he wouldn't be visible if he stayed close to the dark trunks of the trees. In the few spots where the light got in, it illuminated old headstones, one bench, and a couple of historical markers. The rest of the park was blanketed in black. He wondered if Eddie was close to the mark, which was why she didn't text him back. He took more steps in, and farther still. A twig snapped across the park, and DJ gasped. He stood like a statue as time passed, and it was quiet—silent.

DJ turned and hunched over his phone, hoping it would block the screen's glow. He texted, Eddie! Where are you?

A second later there was a buzz a few feet away, and DJ saw an old doll some kid had left in the park, and the silhouette of a small headstone. It was backlit by the glow from the screen of Eddie's phone, lying in the grass. There was a rustling to his right, and he saw a dark shape, bigger than Eddie, move through one of the dim pools of light. Gripped with terror, DJ ran. For a while he wasn't aware of anything except running, until he tripped over a low brick wall and face-planted in someone's garden. It snapped him out of his panic.

His first thought was of his friend and the guilt he felt for running. "Oh, Eddie." He got to his knees and surveyed his surroundings. He was in someone's backyard. There weren't any lights on, but he could make out a patio and shapes of lawn furniture. Panting, he said to himself, "I panicked and ran." He added, "Like a coward."

DJ tried to get his bearings so he'd know which way to go. He figured that if he ran straight out of the park, he'd have run in the direction of his neighborhood, so maybe he was somewhere between the cemetery park and his house.

Another wave of guilt struck him, and DJ punched his thigh. "I don't care how much trouble I get in, I'm calling the police."

He reached in his pocket, but his phone wasn't there. He checked his other pockets, but nothing. He must have dropped it when he freaked and ran. Getting to his feet, he rushed to the back door of the house. He banged on it, calling out for help. After thirty seconds without any response or house lights coming on, he figured the people weren't home. Taking a breath, he ran around the house, across the front lawn, and into the road. He recognized the street, Woodvale.

"I'm almost home. A lot closer to home than the park."

He decided to run home and call the police from their landline. "Mom can ground me for life; I don't care."

He heard someone take a couple of steps on leaves. DJ turned one way and then another, not sure which direction it came from. And then he was off. He flew through the yard of that young couple who didn't have kids, and then through the McGintys'. He hit another street and then plunged into the woods. He'd taken this path at least once a day his whole life, so he knew it by heart and didn't slow a bit in the darkness. Ignoring a painful stitch in his side, he got through the trees in less than a minute and stepped into his own backyard. He started for the back door but changed his mind. If Popper really was following him, he'd see DJ go in and know which house was his. Instead, he ran around front and went in through the front door.

Figuring Popper would notice if he turned on any lights, he left the house dark. He ran down the hallway and into the dark kitchen to peer out the bay window at the way he'd come. The backyard was dark, deeply shadowed, and empty—wonderfully, blessedly empty. DJ stayed at the window until his breathing slowed and his heart stopped pounding.

DJ picked up the landline phone mounted on the kitchen wall, but put it back when he remembered that he hadn't locked the front door. First things first. He ran back down the dark hallway to the front of the house and turned the lock on the doorknob, threw the dead bolt, and actually breathed a sigh of relief.

Reaching for the light switch by the door, he froze at the cheerful voice that came from the dark behind him.

"Do you like Edgar Allan Puh-puh-puh-Poe?"

– CHAPTER 12 –

THE DOLL ROOM

The black Cadillac SUV pulled into the driveway of the Van Werner estate and came to a stop in front of the mansion. The driver's side door opened, and an expressionless man with a shaved head and a black suit exited. He walked to the other side of the vehicle and opened the back door. A young woman got out, reached in for an expensive purse, and pulled it over her shoulder. She took a moment to brush away wrinkles on her business attire: a gray wool skirt with matching jacket, a white button-down shirt, and black high-heeled shoes. She then patted her expensively coiffed, shoulder-length brown hair and reached back into the vehicle to get a clipboard.

She walked past the driver without looking at him and met another woman in business attire standing on the walkway that led to the door of the home.

The woman held out her hand. Her other arm also cradled a clipboard. "Ms. Hunsucker, hi, I'm Jill Morgan. I'll be handling the estate auction next week."

"Ms. Morgan," the new arrival said in a clipped tone. "I'm afraid I'm on a tight schedule." She pronounced the word *shed-ule*. "I'd be appreciative if you could take me right to the doll room."

"Of course, follow me."

Ms. Hunsucker kept one pace behind Ms. Morgan as they made their way up to the doorway of the late-nineteenth-century house. Built in a Gothic revival style, with high-pitched roofs, steep cross gables, and overhanging eaves, a picture of it could easily serve as a book cover for a haunted-house novel.

"I understand the doll collection will be auctioned separately," Ms. Hunsucker said.

"Yes. There will be three auctions. The first for Mr. Van Werner's extensive doll collection. The second will be for his collection of antique automobiles. The third for the remaining articles from his house." She glanced at Ms. Hunsucker when they reached the door. "You're quite young to be Mr. Jernigan's aide-de-camp, aren't you?"

"That depends on what you mean by young. I'm twenty-four, though I know I appear younger. Mr. Jernigan hired me straight out of college when I was twenty-one." That lie flew from her lips with ease. She was, in fact, ten years younger than her professed age of twenty-four. Dressed normally, without a disguise, she looked older than a fourteen-year-old. Many took her to be seventeen or eighteen. But when she threw on the proper clothes, wig, attitude, and tone of voice, she could fool most people, like Ms. Morgan, into believing she was in her twenties. Another lie was the name, Ms. Hunsucker. It was an alias. Her real name's not important, but years ago, because of her prowess on a skateboard, her friends starting calling her Hawk, after the famous skateboarder Tony Hawk.

They entered the house, the sound of their heels like castanets in the cavernous foyer.

As she led Hawk up a curved staircase, Ms. Morgan said, "I had no idea that Lloyd Jernigan was a doll collector."

"Mr. Jernigan," Hawk emphasized *Mr.*, as if she, or Ms. Hunsucker, disapproved of Ms. Morgan using his first name, "feels it is a passion that should be kept secret. His world, the world of finance, is very cutthroat, and some of his rivals and competitors might think that a man who collects dolls is weak." They reached the top of the stairs, and to further solidify her role, she reached for Ms. Morgan's wrist and stopped her. "I hope that you will keep Mr. Jernigan's—oh, shall we say—little hobby between us and no one else."

"Yes, yes, of course."

They started walking again.

Hawk said, "Mr. Jernigan is quite an aggressive collector. He has over two dozen of the rarest dolls, and his crown jewel is one of five original Madame Alexander Eloise dolls still in existence."

"I'm sorry," Ms. Morgan said. "While I've researched the dolls in the Van Werner collection, I'm not familiar with that one."

Hawk calmly said, "Mr. Jernigan paid five million for it."

Ms. Morgan stopped. "Oh my. I'm afraid nothing in Mr. Van Werner's collection is nearly that valuable."

"No, but you are auctioning his Kämmer and Reinhardt, which should sell well into the six figures. And that is the doll Mr. Jernigan is most interested in."

Ms. Morgan pulled a key from her pocket and walked to a nearby door. "Shall we go in?"

"Please."

Ms. Morgan unlocked the door, and they stepped into the doll room. For a moment they stood in darkness, until Ms. Morgan flipped the light switch, bathing the room in a dim glow.

Dizziness struck Hawk. Eyes, hundreds of eyes, watched her from all sides. It was as if she'd been plucked from reality and placed in a nightmare. Something shifted in her peripheral vision, so she turned left. It happened again, and she thought she caught a doll blinking, another doll tilting its head from one side to the other, and then an arm moving. And each time she caught movement, it happened so quickly she had to question if she really saw it. Again, there was subtle movement in the corner of her eye, two dolls putting their heads together as if sharing a secret. Yet, when she turned and looked at them straight on, they were still.

"Are you all right?" Ms. Morgan asked.

It was then that Hawk realized that in her attempt to catch a doll moving, she'd turned in a full circle. "Perfectly. I am just—um—amazed at the size of the Van Werner collection."

"There are three hundred and twenty-six dolls in the collection."

That's six hundred and fifty-two eyes, Hawk thought. "Why is the light so dim?"

"Low light protects the fabric of the dolls' clothes and the paint on the porcelain."

Hawk stepper farther inside, and it seemed that all the dolls' eyes followed her. The little hairs on her neck tingled. The room was large, with shelves covering every wall. She reached out a hand to touch the nearest shelf, noting that all of them, as well as the walls, were covered with pink quilted silk.

"How will you ever auction off so many dolls?" Hawk asked.

"Oh, most will be sold in lots. Several dolls to each lot, dozens in some cases. Only the rarest, like the Kämmer and Reinhardt, will be sold on their own."

Hawk walked around the room. The antique dolls were creepy. Some looked like baby corpses dressed in funeral finery. Others looked demonic. The ones that looked like real babies and toddlers were just as unnerving. The most disturbing was an ancient doll, maybe the oldest in the room. It was filthy, and Hawk felt a wave of déjà vu as she took in its one piercing blue eye, which seemed to be studying her.

She took a breath to steady herself and got to work.

Pretending to appraise the dolls, Hawk shifted her attention to the room itself, looking for security cameras, alarm consoles, motion detectors, and other sensors. There weren't any. The lock to the room had been a simple one, and she noted there was no keyhole or locking mechanism on the inside of the door.

"Ms. Hunsucker? The Kämmer and Reinhardt gets the most honored spot." She led Hawk to a chest-high, glass-fronted antique cabinet.

The doll stood on tiny stockinged feet in a white dress with light blue stitching. White bows tied both pigtails underneath a straw hat.

By tomorrow, Hawk thought, *that will be ours.*

As the black SUV drove off, Hawk yanked off the brown wig. Her actual hair was short and blond.

The bald driver looked at her in the rearview mirror. It was always interesting to look at his eyes. He had a condition known as heterochromia, and his eyes were two different colors, one blue and one brown. "How'd it go, Hawk?"

"Good. But it was eerie, Stan," she answered, kicking off her high heels and wiggling her toes. "I get freaked out by one doll, but a whole roomful? Ugh."

"I don't know why you're scared of dolls, Hawk. Girls are supposed to like dolls."

"Not me; they've always creeped me out. It's a real thing, called pediophobia, the fear of dolls, look it up."

"I'll take your word."

"It's my stepfather's fault. One of my earliest memories from when I was a little kid was when he gave me this dirty old doll he found in the dumpster behind his garage. It had tangled hair, a cracked porcelain face, and one eye—" Hawk's eyes grew wide. That really old one she'd seen in the doll room, it was just like the one her stepfather had given her. A moment later Hawk shook her head, figuring her pediophobia was playing mind games.

"You were saying?" Stan said.

"Oh, sorry. I told my stepfather it was too scary and I didn't want it. I think it made him mad. But he said that was probably for the best, because dolls can come to life. He said that dolls can sense when something terrible or frightening is about to happen; they come to life and walk to where that event will take place so they can watch it happen."

"Your stepfather is a real prince, ain't he?"

Hawk shrugged like it was no big deal, but she remembered how she'd been terrified for weeks after he told her that story, which led to her full-blown pediophobia.

"So, is the job gonna be difficult?"

Hawk smiled. "It's going to be a piece of cake. The doll room door has a simple one-sided lock."

"Do you think she'll try to get in touch with Jernigan to make sure you're legit?"

"I think she bought it. You know, the power of the clipboard."

Stan laughed. He'd taught her that during a con, people always find someone more credible if they're carrying a clipboard.

"Even if she's suspicious, good luck trying to get through to one of the richest men on Wall Street," Stan said. "Imagine, someone believing a man like Lloyd Jernigan collects dollies, one of which is going to earn us a lot of money."

Hawk had met Stan over a year earlier, when he moved into the apartment building across the street from her stepfather's gas station. Her mother had died a couple of years earlier. Other than planting the seeds for her fear of dolls, her stepfather wasn't mean to her, but he did little more than provide food, clothing, and a roof over her head.

Hawk loved skateboarding. In the yard next to the gas station, she'd installed a rail and built a half-pipe ramp, two ramps facing each other in a U-shape. She also used it to hone her mountain bike tricks. Against that side of the gas station, she'd used varying sizes of wood blocks to make her own climbing wall all the way to the top of the second story.

One day she was working on a complicated skateboard maneuver called a darkslide. After a couple dozen fails, she got it right. When she rode down the rail, she heard someone clapping. Across the street, on a second-floor balcony, a bald man sat at a small bistro table applauding. He picked up a coffee cup and held it up in a salute.

Over the next few weeks, he'd be on the balcony watching her skating, biking, and climbing. At first, she thought he was a creep, but he never tried to speak to her. One day, when he was out, she pushed her skateboard across the street and stopped under his balcony. He leaned casually on the railing, looking down.

She studied him and then asked, "What's with the eyes?"

"When I was born, I couldn't decide if I wanted blue eyes or brown, so I took one of each." When she didn't even crack a smile, he said, "It's something I was born with, like a birthmark. I'm Stan, by the way. What's your name?"

"Hawk."

"You're an adrenaline junkie, aren't you?"

"Huh?"

"You like the rush of adrenaline. It's why you do all those stunts and climb that wall."

"I guess so."

Over the next several weeks, they talked more. Her on the sidewalk and him up on his balcony. He talked to her on an even keel, like she was an adult. It was kind of like they were becoming friends. One day, as they were talking, she told him about a play she was doing at school. It was a small cast, and each member acted in several roles. She was surprised when, on opening night, he was in the audience.

The next morning, a Saturday, as she left the apartment over the gas station, Stan called to her from his balcony. "You were good in that play last night."

"Thanks."

"You played, what, four or five different people?"

"Five."

"Right. And every part you did, as different as they were, was believable." He paused, looking her in the eyes. "I got a business proposition for you. Want to come up and discuss it?"

Hawk didn't answer.

"Right, right, stranger danger. How about we talk at Linda's." He nodded up the street to the coffee shop. "I'll buy you a Danish."

They took an outside table.

He sipped his coffee, his eyes on her over the rim. He put it down and said, "You have skills. Skills that could make you a lot of money. You're fearless. You're smart. You crave excitement, that adrenaline burst, and you can act." He drummed his fingers on the tabletop. "Can I trust you, Hawk? I mean, tell you something completely confidential?"

"Yeah, I guess."

"I'm a con artist. You know what that is?" he asked.

"Sure. You con people out of money."

"That's the basic definition, but it goes much deeper. I think you have what it takes to be a good con artist, a great one even. I propose that we become partners. I'll teach you the tricks of the trade, and you won't find a better teacher."

He made it sound like they'd be more like Robin Hood than criminals. "We'll only go after people with lots of money. Money they probably got from scamming people themselves."

When he went on to tell her about some of the past cons he'd worked, she started to warm to the idea, to the excitement, and finally agreed.

A few weeks later, he told her, "We're not crooks, not like robbers or burglars. But on some jobs, those skills can come in handy." He taught her how to pick locks and gave her a lock-picking kit.

He was amazed at how quickly she picked up the skills, and a few months after starting, Hawk ran her first con in the park. They went to the park and set up a table, and he stood aside as she used the sleight-of-hand card game three-card monte to make several hundred dollars. From there they moved on to a classic con known as the Fiddle Game, but they used a fake wedding ring instead of a phony, valuable violin. A little more complicated than three-card monte, it involved Hawk playing a naive kid and Stan acting as a passing jeweler. The mark was a man who owned a number of apartment buildings and was well known for his greed. Hawk pretended to find the ring in the parking lot at the man's office and asked, when he stepped out of the office, if he knew of anyone who lost a ring with a big diamond in it. Stan, the fake jeweler, happened by, overheard them, and looked at the ring. Then, out of Hawk's earshot, he told the man the ring was worth tens of thousands of dollars and then left. The man persuaded Hawk to sell him the ring for three thousand, a fraction of what Stan told him it was worth. The ring's actual value, as a fake, was right around five bucks, so a nice profit on her second con.

They worked other cons, like the Jersey Sleigh Ride, the Devil's Temptation, and the Newspaper Shuffle. The only rough patch in their relationship was when Stan wanted to work a con on a rich, old widow, and Hawk refused. She had met the woman in the initial setup and found she was a sweet, trusting widow who used her money to fund a number of charities. Stan had lost his temper, had said some cruel things, and they went a month and a half without talking.

It was Stan who reached out to her. He apologized for the things he said and wanted to know if Hawk was up for a new job involving valuable dolls. A little different than past jobs, it would consist of one part con and one part burglary.

A little after one AM, Stan, now driving a nondescript gray sedan, dropped Hawk off at the end of the driveway leading to the Van Werner estate. She wore all black, from her sneakers to her stocking cap. She slung a small backpack over her shoulder and disappeared into the shadows of the trees that lined the drive. Ten minutes later she stood on the stoop of the back door, or one of the back doors. The house was so big it had five entrances, and two could count as back doors. She got out her lock-picking kit and silently counted off the seconds as she worked on the lock. At twenty-three, she had it opened. Hawk moved swiftly and silently through the darkness toward the staircase.

On the second floor, tall, ornate windows lined the left-side wall, and muted moonglow filtered in, illuminating the checkerboard pattern tiles on the floor. Continuing down the hall, she stopped at the door to the doll room. Once again, she did her magic with the lockpicks.

The room was darker than the hallway. Hawk pulled a small LED flashlight from her backpack and switched it on, revealing fast movement along the floor. Something bumped into her right foot, and she lifted it with a squeal. Something hit her left ankle even harder, and she lost her balance, stumbling back a couple of steps into the hall-way before falling and hitting her head against a window frame. Stunned, her vision blurred, she couldn't make out anything taking place around her. There were sounds, though. Scurrying and hushed, childlike whispers. Her flashlight lay on the floor ten feet away and cast its beam down the long, dark hallway. Hawk scrambled across the floor and snatched it up. On her knees, she swept the flashlight around. Nothing was out of the ordinary.

Hawk aimed her light at the open doorway to the doll room, but from that angle, she couldn't see in. She wondered if her imagination worked together with her fear of dolls to make her conjure up what she'd experienced. That didn't seem right. She'd always been so grounded, and not one to succumb to flights of fancy. Hawk decided right then that it was time to pull it together, grab the doll, and leave. Getting to her feet, she peered around the doorframe into the doll room. Hundreds of dolls were perched on shelves.

She shook her head, knowing she'd acted like an idiot. Yeah, dolls were creepy, but dolls weren't alive; they weren't able to move, or walk, or whisper. Entering, she went to the cabinet holding the Kämmer and Reinhardt. Quick work with the lockpick opened it. The doll's porcelain face stared out expressionlessly with faint blue eyes and full faded red lips. Hawk smiled as she reached for the doll—and it smiled back. Tiny blue eyes shifted to focus on her.

Screaming, Hawk knocked into shelves, sending numerous dolls to the floor. When she aimed her flashlight there, dolls twitched and jerked as they got to their feet and turned their painted eyes up to her. More dolls climbed down from their perches to the floor. Hawk ran from the doll room, at some point dropping her flashlight. At the top of the stairs, a shadow shifted from the darkness and moved at her. Hands grabbed her arms, and she screamed.

"Hawk, Hawk, it's me, Stan."

"Stan? Why? What?"

"Are you all right? You're screaming and running and acting all crazy."

"Stan? Is it really you?" Her hands went up and felt at his face.

A second later Stan turned on a flashlight and aimed it at himself. "It's me, Hawk. See?"

Panting, she tried to explain. "We have to get out of here, Stan. They're alive. I saw them moving and smiling and walking and—and—"

"Calm down, Hawk. It's the dark and your fear of dolls, that's all. It went to your head."

"I swear, Stan. They're alive. They knocked me off my feet."

"I'm here now. We'll go to the doll room, grab that doll, and get out. Won't take but a few seconds."

Hawk shook her head. "I don't know, Stan. I mean—"

"Come on, kid, pull yourself together. Ten seconds, in and out."

"Okay, okay."

Stan put an arm over her shoulders and led her back toward the doll room.

"Why are you here, Stan? You weren't supposed to come in. It wasn't in the plan."

"I got worried about you is all. Turned out I was right, huh?" Stan pointed his light into the doll room. "Dang, kid. You really did a number in here."

The majority of the dolls lay scattered about the floor. "It wasn't me, Stan. I swear it."

"Come on." He grabbed her arm, squeezing a little too tight, and led her into the room. His flashlight lit up the cabinet. "Is that it? That where they're keeping my payday?"

"Yeah, Stan. But it looked at me. It smiled at me."

Kicking dolls out of the way, Stan pulled her after him and stopped before the open cabinet door. He reached in and grabbed the valuable doll. A second later Stan smiled at Hawk, his eyes narrowed as his smile slipped into a sneer, and he shoved Hawk into a corner. She hit the shelves hard and fell to her knees. Before she could make sense of what happened and get to her feet, the door closed with a click, followed by the sound of Stan's own lockpicks.

"No, Stan! No!" Now she was in total darkness, and her tears fell freely. She stumbled through the dolls, nearly losing her footing, and made it to the door. She tried the doorknob, but Stan had already locked it.

"Stan!" Hawk screamed.

From the other side of the door, Stan said, "You shoulda done the widow job, Hawk." His voice sounded calm on the surface, but she heard an undercurrent of anger. "You shoulda done what I told you. This is your fault, kiddo."

"Stan, no!"

"Payday on this job is just too big. I don't want to share."

"Stan, please. Let me out. Don't leave me in here with the dolls."

"Don't worry. Someone will be here in the morning to let you out. Of course, you'll also get arrested when they find you."

Breathing hard, she felt anger ignite in her chest, and she shouted, "I can tell them about you! I will! I'll turn you in!"

Stan chuckled. "Tell them what? You know a man named Stan who taught you how to be a con artist? You don't even know my real name, Hawk. I've been conning you this whole time. From the first time I saw you on your skateboard, I've been working you. And by the time the police show up at my apartment, I'll be long gone. See ya, kiddo. Enjoy juvie."

"Stan! No, Stan!" Hawk pleaded, sobbing uncontrollably. "You can keep the money, Stan. All of it. Just let me out!" She stopped to take a breath and heard something even worse: the subtle sound of dolls moving.

On the day of the auction, Hawk once again put on Ms. Hunsucker's wig and business suit. She hired a car and driver to take her to the Van Werner estate. Returning like that, without knowing what had happened the rest of that night, went against everything Stan had taught her about being a con artist. But she had gone on the auction house website, and they still claimed to be selling the Kämmer and Reinhardt doll, even though Stan had taken it. How? She had to know.

In the back of her hired car, she thought about Stan. He'd turned out to be a greedy, traitorous backstabber. After he'd locked her in the doll room and left, she first heard the sound of moving dolls and then felt their little hands and arms as they grasped at her. She panicked and ran in the dark, straight into a wall. It was then she'd lost consciousness, though she wasn't sure if it was from the impact or from intense fear.

"You all right? You're looking a little pale." The driver looked at her in the rearview mirror.

"I'm fine. Please pay attention to the road."

"Yes, ma'am."

After running into the wall, the next thing she remembered was waking up to morning sunshine. She was outside and under a bush. All around her in the dirt were little footprints, the size dolls would make.

Hawk didn't know what happened to Stan. She went straight to his apartment, thinking he would have already taken all his belongings and left, but his possessions were still there, including all the money he kept hidden in a small room behind a bookcase.

Hawk had studied the newspapers and watched the news over the next several days, but there was no mention of a burglary at the Van Werner estate. After checking the auction house website the day before, she couldn't resist the temptation to return in the guise of Ms. Hunsucker.

Ms. Morgan was standing outside the open door of the Van Werner home, welcoming bidders for the upcoming auction. As before, she held a clipboard, and under that she also had a doll in hand.

She turned from a couple who were entering the mansion and saw Hawk. "Ms. Hunsucker, so happy to have you here."

"I'm afraid I have some bad news. Mr. Jernigan will not be bidding after all," Hawk said, having planned out a viable excuse for her being there.

Ms. Morgan's expression turned to one of alarm. "Oh no. He's not questioning the authenticity of the Kämmer and Reinhardt, is he?"

"No, nothing like that," Hawk said. "Between you and me, he's had a difficult couple of weeks and feels it is not a good idea to spend a large amount of money right now."

"I understand. But you've come anyway?"

"I was in the area and thought I'd come and tell you myself."

Ms. Morgan smiled. "How very kind."

Hawk plunged into the real reason she'd come. "So the auction will go ahead as planned?"

"Of course. And the Kämmer and Reinhardt doll will be the final sale."

How? Hawk thought, and then asked, "Have you seen it lately, the doll?"

"Yes, we moved the entire inventory into another room next to where the auction will be held. Why?"

Hawk gave her a shrug and a smile. Before Ms. Morgan had time to get suspicious, she changed the topic and pointed to the doll she held under her clipboard. "Is that another you'll be selling?"

Ms. Morgan looked at the doll and said, "No. Though we inventoried the doll room twice, we missed this one both times. Neither of our experts recognized it, and both felt it's of no value, so I was taking it for my niece. Is it one you recognize?"

She handed the doll over. Hawk looked at it and felt as if she'd plunged into ice-cold water. The doll was male. A figure in a black suit with a bald porcelain head. One of the doll's eyes was blue and the other was brown, and they shifted to look at Hawk. Its mouth opened wide in a silent scream, and she dropped it.

"Ms. Hunsucker? Are you okay, Ms. Hunsucker?" Ms. Morgan called after Hawk as she ran to the car.

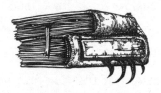

CHAPTER 13

THE HOUSE OF MYSTERY AND MIRRORS (PART 3)

Jana added an echo effect to the last line of *The Doll Room* so the words reverberated as she brought up the calliope music bed. It was time to finish my own personal odd occurrence.

I woke up in my bed with no clue as to how I'd gotten home. The last thing I remembered was stepping from the door of the House of Mystery and Mirrors and putting my foot on the porch.

I plugged the charger into my phone to check the date.

Though it felt as if I'd been away for months, it was only the morning after Tobin and I had gone to the carnival. I brought up my contact list and called Tobin. A recorded voice told me it was not a working number. I tried three more times with the same result.

Both my parents had already left for work. I hopped on my bike and rode to Tobin's house. Nobody was home, but I got the spare key they kept under a flowerpot and let myself in. I ran upstairs and into Tobin's room. It was empty; there was no furniture, no posters, no clothes in the closet. I knew what was happening, but it didn't lessen my panic. I got on my bike and rode out to the special-events field. The carnival was gone, and there was no evidence that it had ever been there.

I raced back to Tobin's house. This time Jana was there, having just returned from visiting her grandparents, but she didn't believe me when I told her about the carnival. Anger, panic, and fear followed me as I tried to find proof that Tobin was real and existed.

I grabbed my microphone and readjusted it so I could keep talking as I leaned forward, both elbows on the table. I was exhausted and emotional.

"Tobin is still there, in the House of Mystery and Mirrors."

I had to stop because my voice broke. I was close to crying. "Waiting for us to come get him, or maybe he's older, or ancient." I swallowed. "Or worse."

Jana did cry, wiping at tears on her cheeks. "Even though I don't remember him, I can't bear the thought that my brother might think we've abandoned him."

I did feel helpless, but there was solace in that we were doing something. "I've kept the map I made of the maze, and it's safe in a hidden location." I looked at the mirror on the wall, on the back of which I'd Velcroed the map. "In an attempt to find that carnival, Jana and I started the *Odd Occurrences* podcast and set up the Carnival Nocturne hotline. But so far, no one has called it. So please, if you see that carnival in your town, call me at 386-555-3822."

I thanked the audience, passed along the Carnival Nocturne hotline number one more time, and bid our listeners good night. Jana killed the mics.

"Whew, I'm beat." I cupped a hand and filled it with water from a bottle and splashed it on my face. After drying off with a paper towel, I checked the time. "It's almost three in the morning."

"I was curious how long the podcast would take. Almost six hours." Jana was shutting down equipment and paused to blow her nose. Her eyes were red from crying. "I think it was an awesome show."

I stretched. "Yeah."

Just then, the calliope music ringtone for the Carnival Nocturne hotline started playing. Jana and I froze. Our eyes locked.

I forced myself to move and answered it on speaker. "Hello?"

There were several seconds of silence, followed by "Hello, Zeus." The voice was deep and smoky, and I recognized it at once. The Queen of the Carnival, the matriarch of the House of Mystery and Mirrors.

I didn't want her to know how her voice frightened me, so I took a breath and spoke softly. "Where's Tobin?"

She laughed like I'd just told her a joke. "You know where he is, Zeus."

Jana looked stunned. She had believed me about Carnival Nocturne and Tobin, only now that belief was solidified when she heard the voice of something that wasn't human.

"Where are you?"

"Zeus."

"Where's the carnival?"

"Zeus."

"Where's the House of Mystery and Mirrors?"

She sighed like my questions bored her. "You've been talking about us, haven't you?"

"Yes."

"Why?" she asked.

"I want Tobin back."

She laughed again. "You know that's not going to happen. Tobin has so much to offer, youth and years and energy—" Her voice dropped into something diabolical. "And his life."

I spoke slowly and enunciated each word. "Where are you?"

"Where we first met, Zeus. We've made a special stop here in Crescent Harbor just for you. You've been looking for us, for Tobin. Come to me now." And then the call ended.

"They're back," I said, staring blankly.

Jana blinked several times. "That's—wow—that's scary, Zeus."

"We're going to get Tobin back."

Jana nodded with grim determination.

We'd had a year to plan. It seemed like a good strategy, but now that we were putting it into action, I was having doubts.

Jana was all business and took the mirror hanging on the wall and flipped it over to the map I'd made of the maze. "Here. Keep it safe."

I'd been to the beach a couple of days earlier and still had a towel in my backpack. I used it to wrap the mirror and map, before stashing it in the pack.

Jana brought out our mobile audio recorder. "A little more prep."

We spent a few minutes recording my voice and then started for the special-events field a little after three-fifteen in the morning. I rode my bike, and Jana rode my brother's.

We were silent for most of the trip. I'm sure that Jana, like myself, was mentally going over all the things that could, and probably would, go wrong. We had a half-moon and the occasional streetlight to provide illumination, but it was still a dark and creepy trip. We didn't see a single car or person. A year earlier, Tobin and I had traveled this same route, but we changed it up this time; instead of turning at the first street, we continued on to the woods behind the special-events field. We turned at the next street up, which would take us along the north side of the woods, closest to where the House of Mystery and Mirrors had been erected.

I picked what I thought was the best spot and pointed

into the trees. "Go straight in, that's where you'll find the house. You'll come at it from the back. Stay in the woods and go around it to the west. Find a good spot where you can see the porch. Whatever you do, stay hidden."

She nodded, dropped the bike, and retrieved a small flashlight from her backpack. Earlier at the studio, she'd covered the lenses of our flashlights with packing tape that she pierced with the tip of a pencil. She clicked it on, and the small hole produced a thin beam that wouldn't be nearly as noticeable.

Jana wasn't that affectionate, but she hugged me awkwardly and whispered, "I'll see you soon." She disappeared into the woods.

I continued east until the woods ended at the field's parking area. I turned in and rode to where Carnival Nocturne had set up the first time. I parked my bike and stopped for just a second before the burgundy rope strung across the entrance. I yanked it free, and it dropped to the ground. There were no ticket booths or tents, and no paper lanterns lighting the way. But I wasn't alone. The Exceptionals, the Queen's army, lined up along either side of the carnival thoroughfare and made no move to stop me. I tried to look like I wasn't scared. I kept my head held high as I passed Big Guy.

Next was the two-headed man. "You're toast, kiddo," Winston said.

Hume's head nodded.

Frog Boy stared at me but was momentarily distracted by a buzzing insect. His tongue shot out and snagged it. His eyes returned to me as he chewed.

They could have grabbed and overpowered me as soon as I'd arrived, but I'd counted on the Queen's conceit, her belief that she was all powerful. It would, hopefully, provide me the slightest chance. I'd see her soon enough, where she waited, biding her time like a black widow in her web.

At the crossroads, I turned right. There were no more Exceptionals; it was just me, alone, in the woods at night, going to meet a vampire that consumed years instead of blood. It was a long, dark walk, my doubts growing with each step. I was a kid, and she was a supernatural entity. My plan was based on nothing but guesses and conjecture. I'm sure that doubting myself was what she was hoping for. She wanted me hesitant, uncertain, and scared. And I was all those things, but with Tobin in the mirrors, I had no choice. He was, as Dad liked to say, my brother from another mother.

Rounding a curve, I saw the porch light of the House

of Mystery and Mirrors. I paused to get my flashlight. I stepped into the trees and turned it on, slowly making my way around the back of the house. I took my time, surveying the ground to make sure I wouldn't step on anything that made noise. Finally, I approached the back corner of the house, which was on the opposite side from where Tobin and I saw the Queen of the Carnival in the rocking chair. I held up my flashlight and flicked it on and off three times. My signal to Jana.

I heard my own voice calling from the woods in front of the house, "*Hello.*"

Just one of several things I'd said into our mobile digital recorder before leaving the studio. I crept up along the side of the house and peeked up onto the porch. The Queen, in her beautiful disguise, rose from her rocking chair.

"Zeus, you did come. Such a brave boy." When there was no response, the Queen strode to the porch stairs. "Don't be shy, Zeus."

Jana played my recorded voice. "*Where's Tobin?*"

"Oh, you know where he is. Why don't you come look for him?"

We figured she would say something along those lines, and I'd recorded what Jana played next. "*You come look for me.*"

The Queen's head twitched, and though her smile remained, I could also see traces of anger in her narrowed eyes. I wanted her furious. She'd be more likely to make mistakes.

She went down the porch steps and stopped. "Don't try my patience, Zeus."

Jana had also recorded me laughing, and she played that. It did the trick, because the Queen stormed out to the streetlight.

"Where are you, Zeus?"

As the Queen peered into the dark woods, I climbed up and slipped over the railing. Staying low, I made my way across the porch.

"*You were beautiful when I first saw you,*" my recording said.

"Thank you very much, Zeus."

"*But now I see you for what you are. Evil and ugly.*"

"Sticks and stones," the Queen said.

When I got to the door, I put my hand on the knob and waited for Jana. A second later she played me shouting, "*TELL ME NOW, WHERE'S TOBIN?*"

I turned the knob right then so the Queen wouldn't hear the door opening. I slid in and silently shut the door. Jana's job was done. I just hoped she'd make it back to the studio safely. As I stood in the foyer, mirrors rose from the floor to the ceiling. Taking the map with the mirror backing from my knapsack, I started into the labyrinth. It had taken Tobin and me hours to make our way through the maze that first time, but with the map, I traversed the mirrors in twenty minutes. I stepped through the portal mirror with the exit sign buzzing above it. Returning the map to my backpack, I felt like I had never left. I went down hallways and took stairs higher. On the fifth floor, I rounded a corner into another corridor, and a figure came charging at me, knocking me onto my back. As I regained my senses, I gazed up at a smiling face.

"Dude, it's so good to see you," Tobin said, straddling my waist. He stood and helped me up.

I gave him a big hug. "How are you?"

"Doing okay for someone who's been stuck here forever. I was looking out the vent when you started calling to the Queen, but I didn't see you cross the yard to come in."

I told him how Jana and I had fooled the Queen. I looked at him closely. "You're not any older."

"They haven't found our hiding place yet." His smile fell. "I can't believe you came back."

"I have the map," I said. "We'll get out this time. Both

of us. And we'll take as many of the kids trapped here as we can find."

"No telling when they'll hunt again. Let's head up to the attic."

On the way up, he told me how he'd attempted to backtrack when we'd split up in my escape and his failed attempt. "It was like the first time we went through: I ended up lost, and after hours of wandering around, I finally found the portal mirror."

"I don't know what happened when I stepped out the door. I was going to come back for you, but first I went out on the porch, and the next thing I knew, I was in bed at home, and it was the next morning. When I went back to the special-events field, the carnival was gone. Man, I'm so sorry, Tobin."

"Don't apologize. I knew you wouldn't abandon me."

Back in the attic, we sat and talked. "How long have I been in the mirrors?"

"A year. Tonight's Halloween."

"Really? A year? Seems so much longer than that." He looked down and asked, "Does my family miss me?"

I put a hand on his shoulder. "It's like Kid said, anyone in here is forgotten out there. I think I still remembered you because I'd been inside here with you. The only person who believed me was Jana. Even though she can't remember you, she helped me find the carnival again."

"Of course she did—she's fearless, and also the best sister a kid could have."

I told him about creating the podcast for the ultimate goal of locating Carnival Nocturne, not expecting that it would return to Crescent Harbor.

"So Jana was messing with the Queen?" Tobin laughed.

"By now she should have left. We'll meet up with her later."

He grinned and shook his head. "Can't believe you're here." He hugged me again.

We wandered the halls and rooms of the House of Mystery and Mirrors, letting the other kids know that we'd be leaving soon and they were free to join us. They stared at me like I was a rock star. Not only was I the kid who got away, but now I'd come back to help them. Word spread, and soon the plan was to meet at the portal mirror. Tobin and I returned to the attic. Out of habit, I sat in the chair by the vent and looked out.

"Here they come."

Tobin stood next to me as the Queen crossed the yard toward the front door. Frog Boy followed, and behind him Big Guy, grasping a girl's arm and pulling her along.

"Oh no, they have Jana."

"I figured they'd come after me. But catching Jana wasn't part of the plan." I thought a moment and ran through our strategy again. "Doesn't matter; it can still work."

"What can work?"

"You'll see."

I ran, and Tobin followed in confusion. "What are you doing, Zeus?"

"Trust me," I nearly shouted. I continued speaking loudly, saying things like, "It'll be okay." And, "They'll never find us."

It was on the seventh floor that we heard the familiar ping of the Queen's echolocation. I pulled Tobin through a nearby door into a room littered with broken furniture. He watched as I took off my backpack.

I got out the mirror, flipped it over, removed the map from the back, and handed it to him. "If anything happens to me, use it to get everyone out."

His expression screamed *I don't understand*, and then we heard them out in the hallway. I returned the mirror to the backpack and ran out the door and into the arms of Big Guy.

Big Guy held me above the ground so that we were eye to eye. I didn't struggle, because it was my plan to get caught. He dropped me next to Frog Boy, a smile on his wide froggy lips. I got to my feet.

"Look who we found wandering through the woods near the House of Mystery and Mirrors," the Queen said in her hideous form.

Jana's jaw was slack, and she gazed out with blank eyes.

I rushed toward her, but the Queen held up her hand, fingers spasming, and I no longer had control of my body. My feet stopped, but momentum carried me forward and down onto my face. I couldn't even bring up my arms to block my fall.

"Stand up," the Queen said.

I got to my feet, and blood flowed from one of my nostrils. I wanted to wipe it away, but neither of my hands worked.

Somehow, I found my voice. "Leave her alone."

The Queen stared at me with wide eyes. "He spoke, Falstaff. Zeus is a strong one and will feed us well."

I opened my mouth to say something, but she twitched a finger and my lips closed tight. My mind worked fine, but my body was no longer in my control.

"Come, Zeus. You too, Jana." She turned, and Jana and I

followed. Frog Boy hopped to our right; Big Guy tramped along on our left.

It was a strange feeling being under someone's influence. I told my legs to stop, but they just marched along. I wanted to look at Jana to make sure she was okay, but I couldn't turn my head. As we navigated the halls, I knew that if I was under the Queen's spell, I faced the possibility of losing years from my life.

We approached the Domed Chamber. Big Guy opened both doors, stood to the side, and gave me an *after you* gesture. I'm sure I looked calm, maybe even bored, but on the inside, I was panicking. The deep, rhythmic throbbing of the Black Mirror greeted us, coming every three seconds. Pressure swelled in my chest with each pulse and got more potent the closer we were to it. We stopped twenty feet from the center of the room.

The Queen stepped past me and turned. "We'll let your friend go first, Zeus, so you can see what's in store for you." She walked slowly backward, using her index finger to beckon Jana.

Jana stepped into my peripheral view, and my hand shot out and grabbed her arm, stopping her. The Queen looked at me with concern. A second later Jana pulled free and started for the Black Mirror.

Mustering as much willpower as I could, I shouted, "WAIT!" It was like trying to speak with my jaw wired shut. "I'll go first."

Big Guy approached me, raising his enormous hammer.

"No, Falstaff," the Queen said. He lowered the hammer. "Zeus, if you want to go first, I'll accommodate you."

The Queen and I approached the center of the room. She pulled the canvas from the mirror like a matador waving his cape at a bull. Mounted on claw-foot legs, the Black Mirror faced the other direction. The Queen took my hand, led me to the other side, and stood me right in front.

She moved behind me and whispered in my ear, "Kids usually last three or maybe four times in front of the mirror before all life is drained. Because you are someone special, someone who escaped and talks about us to the world, this will be your only time in front of the mirror. You will stand here, Zeus, the years pulled from your young life, until you're no longer young, until you die."

She stroked my hair as I stared numbly. On the inside, I was screaming in terror.

She stepped away from me and went to stand next to Jana. "Look at the mirror, Zeus."

I did. The glass was black and reminded me of a wet

road. Though I was mainly a puppet and the Queen was pulling my strings, I felt my face constrict with fear. When I'd come up with my plan, I thought there could be two outcomes. One, it would work, or two, if it didn't work, I'd lose years of my life, which was bad. But now my life was on the line.

Transfixed before the mirror, I thought about her look of surprise when I spoke and again when I grabbed Jana's arm. Maybe, just maybe, her power had limits. If I worked at it, perhaps I could at least move my arms. As I tried, the mirror started to lighten, from black to dark gray. I saw a figure. As it lightened more, I recognized myself in that dim reflection. Finally, it looked like an ordinary mirror. Then things changed. My reflection swirled. It took me back to art class in elementary school, when the teacher had mounted art paper to spinning turntables, and we'd drizzle paint onto it, creating circular designs.

I saw lots of things in the mirror, bursts of colored light, rivers of fire, a thousand eyes watching and blinking as one, and images of people who flashed so quickly that they seemed a blur. I knew that what the mirror showed were all the kids who had faced the Black Mirror in the past. The mirror returned to its original black state, and that was when pain struck. It felt like hundreds of long needles were pushing into my arms and legs. My torso was on fire, and I feared my head would split in two, if not explode. Kid said the pain was as bad as an amputation without anesthesia. To me, it felt like my body was being slowly ripped apart.

Now! I thought to myself. *Force yourself to move now or you'll never have another chance!* Hundreds of pounds of pressure weighed on me from all sides as I worked to remove my backpack. I moved slowly, like I was encased in gelatin; it took immense concentration.

The Queen laughed at my efforts, but I finally held my backpack. Focusing again, I struggled to remove my mirror. *Fight fire with fire*, I thought.

"What is he doing?" Falstaff asked.

Frog Boy croaked.

"It doesn't matter what he does," the Queen said.

I dropped the backpack and held my mirror in both hands. *Raise the mirror*, I thought. And my arms slowly rose. *Higher.* I managed to bring up my mirror so that it was directly in front of my eyes and facing the Black Mirror. When that happened, the throbbing in the room shifted into a sound like a hundred tuning forks struck at the same time, ranging in pitch from ultra-high to the deepest timbre imaginable and all notes in between. It was soft at first but quickly grew until the sound resonated around the room at a volume that matched a jet engine roaring at takeoff.

The all-encompassing pain ended. I wavered, almost falling to the ground in blessed relief. The Queen no longer had me under her control. The Black Mirror reflected the mirror I held. I was not in the reflection, nor was any other part of the room. The mirror image dimmed and brightened repeatedly. My idea, my theory, was that if the Black Mirror leeched power and energy from those facing it, then a mirror placed in front of it, creating a reflection of a reflection, would suck power and energy from the Black Mirror, and ultimately from the Queen.

She shrieked, "What are you doing?"

There was a sound like a suction cup being pulled from glass, and a wispy form was pulled from the Black Mirror and flew into mine. Then another and another, over and over, faster and faster, the suction sound accompanying each.

Looking to the side, I saw the Queen grasping Jana's shoulders with both hands and struggling to stay on her feet. The plan Jana and I had devised was working, and working faster than I could have hoped. My mirror started bouncing and twisting. It was hard to hold steady.

She was no longer strong enough to shout, so I couldn't hear her, but I read her lips as she said, "Stop himmmmmm." The Queen had been hideous before, but she was now shrinking in on herself like a rotting apple, her head wobbling on her neck.

Big Guy struggled to hold the big sledgehammer as he rapidly aged. He took a step toward me, his sledge-hammer raised. In the next instant, he seemed a century older and the sledgehammer slipped from his grasp and dropped to the floor. He managed another step before he fell to his knees and swayed back and forth. As the Queen lost her power, the immortality she shared with The Exceptionals was gone. They were rapidly growing older, to their true age. Big Guy's flesh turned into old, cracked leather, and then he dried out to a paperlike texture, which flaked from his skeleton. He was dead before falling forward, his skull breaking apart on impact.

Sobbing, the Queen, too, aged. Wrinkles ran over her white flesh like cracks in a coffee mug.

My mirror was hot now, smoke rising as it shook.

Frog Boy hopped into view, and appeared mummified. He took another hop and splatted onto the floor, his limbs splayed.

The Queen stumbled toward me. I stood still as she approached. Her flesh continued to wrinkle and dry out with each passing second. She reached me and fell to her knees. Wrapping her arms around my legs, she looked up at me, the darkness around her eyes and mouth spreading. "Please, spare me." Black tears leaked from her eyes. She willed herself to smile. "I promise that if you stop, you can join me and we will live forever."

I stepped from her grasp and lowered the mirror. The noise lessened. "Forever?"

She held her arms up toward me, pleadingly. "Yesss, yesss. I make that vow on this Halloween night."

"Trick-or-treat," I said, and held up the mirror again.

When the deafening rumble blared anew, she screamed, pitched face forward, and broke into dust when she struck the ground.

My mirror cooled and stopped shaking and the blasting sound stopped, but the Black Mirror smoked and vibrated. Cracks showed on its surface, and a second later it shattered into a thousand tiny pieces that tore across the room. I dropped to the floor and covered my head with my arms, feeling stings where I was struck. Next, I heard crackling all around me, not like breaking glass, but deeper in tone. I jumped to my feet and looked up.

Wide fissures opened in the dome, and small pieces of the ceiling fell. Jana stood halfway across the room. I ran and tackled her just as the sound built into a crashing crescendo. The dome blew apart. I sprawled across her body. It was a symphony of crashing, shattering, and smashing as pieces of the dome fell to the ground around us.

The cacophony stopped, and I felt strong hands pull me up. I blinked and saw Tobin smile at me.

"I believe this is yours." He handed me the map and then helped his sister to her feet. Breathing hard, Jana stepped back and studied him, his face, his body, and then his face again.

A joyful grin grew on her lips. "I remember," she whispered. And then she shouted, "Tobin!" She wrapped him up in a fierce hug.

He was laughing his goofy Tobin laugh, and when they pulled apart, I saw tears on both their faces.

We gathered all the kids who'd been stuck in the house, and they followed Tobin, Jana, and me. It was like a parade, everyone excited and laughing and cheering as we made our way to the portal mirror. I hadn't felt this good in a long, long time.

As we came into view of the portal, the floor moved.

"What was that?" Jana asked.

The floor shook, slowly at first, but it quickly grew in strength. It was an earthquake accompanied by a ringing that grew higher in pitch.

"The sound's coming from there." Tobin pointed to the portal mirror. He cautiously approached it and pushed his head through the mirror. A second later he pulled back out and shouted, "RUN!"

Kids ran off in all directions. Tobin caught up to Jana and me and told us what he saw between breaths. "All the mirrors in the maze are vibrating. I think it's going to blow like the Domed Chamber."

A second later there was an explosion so strong that it knocked us off our feet. I hunched into a little ball, but chanced a look up as broken shards of thousands of mirrors flew through the air, slicing the House of Mystery and Mirrors into pieces as easily as if it were made of paper.

"Stay down!" I shouted.

Like a million flying stilettos, jagged splinters of glass whistled as they tore overhead, whittling away the house. I closed my eyes and forced my body into a tighter ball and waited to feel the fatal sting of shredding glass.

It seemed to last an eternity.

We were in the woods near the special-events field. The exact spot where the House of Mystery and Mirrors had stood. No trace of it was left.

"Is it over?"

We turned to the voice, and there was Vince, bald, and looking like he was almost fifty years old.

"I think so," I said.

Vince gazed down at the backs of his hands. "What'll my parents think when they see me like this?"

This time I didn't have an answer for him. Then I noticed it was just us four. "Where are the other kids?"

"I don't know," Tobin said.

"I think I do," Jana said. She pointed at me. "You, me, Tobin, and Vince were taken while the carnival was here in Crescent Harbor. And it's where we returned when the house was destroyed."

I picked up on her theory. "So when the house was destroyed, all those kids returned to where they'd been taken."

"I hope so," Tobin said.

We started through the woods, heading for the special-events field. Both Jana and Tobin kept giving me odd glances.

"What?" I asked.

"Zeus, you're older," Jana said with a whisper.

"And taller," Tobin said in disbelief.

I'd always been taller than Tobin, but Jana and I were eye to eye. Now I looked down on them both. "I wasn't in front of the Black Mirror that long."

"Guess that's all it took, because you look like you're, I don't know, eighteen."

Miraculously, I still held my mirror. I started to bring it up to check my reflection.

Tobin stopped me. "Don't look in that mirror, ever. No telling what would happen after it reflected the Black Mirror."

I nodded and threw it to the ground, where it broke into little pieces.

"Look," Tobin said, pointing at the shards.

Those wispy forms that had been sucked from the Black Mirror into mine rose into the air. One by one, they flew from the remnants of the broken mirror. Their release increased in speed as more left the broken pieces.

"I don't understand," Jana said, watching the forms as they disappeared into the sky.

"Zeus, I think you just released all those kids who died while they were being taken," Tobin said.

I was stunned as I watched the flight of those The Exceptionals had fed on. And I felt like crying because I'd just lost a few years of my life.

Tobin grabbed me by the arms. "What's wrong?"

I looked down at him. "I'm older."

"Zeus, you did it. You freed us. As for being older, well, you'll be my *older* brother from another mother."

– CHAPTER 14 –

SLIVER

"This has been a fun evening," I said into the microphone.

"I'm proud of you, Zeus," Jana said.

"Why?"

She tapped on our wooden table. "This is the first podcast you've done where you didn't knock on wood before you started."

"I've decided I don't want to be superstitious anymore." I gave a little salute to Tobin. "Once again, a hearty welcome to our new cohost."

"Hey, it's been great," Tobin said. "I hope all our *Odd Occurrences* listeners enjoyed my version of what happened on the other side of the mirrors."

Tobin had been funny and expressive, a natural in front of the mic. It had been a week since our Halloween special, and tonight we told our listeners how we got Tobin back and destroyed the House of Mystery and Mirrors. We talked about how it was like he'd never been gone. People knew him, and his room had returned to its natural state of messiness amidst the furniture, posters, and clothes.

After the podcast, Jana took time to shut off the equipment.

Tobin wandered around the studio. "This is really cool. You guys actually got a podcast going."

"It's so much nicer to hear about *Odd Occurrences* and not have to live one," I said.

"You got that right."

When Jana finished, we locked the studio shed and went through my house. I said good night to my parents because I was spending the night at Tobin's. It was a cool evening, and though thousands of stars lit up the sky, it seemed exceptionally dark. We turned onto Tobin and Jana's street. There was a sudden flash of light on the road.

"Did you see that?" Jana asked.

"Yeah, what was it?" I asked and pointed. "Light flared for just a second."

We got to the spot and stood in a circle around an object.

Tobin knelt and picked it up. It was a jagged shard from a broken mirror, almost a foot in length. "How did this get here?"

Jana squinted at it. "It's got to be a coincidence."

I held out my hands, and Tobin placed it across my open palms. As we studied it, the reflection lightened to twilight bright, and we saw movement within it. Strange-looking people, people who would fit in with The Exceptionals, were moving about, carrying lumber, tools, lengths of mirrors, and folded canvas. A figure strode into view. He was a large man, bigger than Big Guy. He had a beard and long black hair.

The man put his hands on his hips and yelled, "Put your backs into it. The sooner it's rebuilt, the sooner we visit Crescent Harbor."

Then he turned and walked toward us until only a closeup of his face was visible in the sliver. Weathered and lined, an ugly scar ran from hairline to beard, separating his face into two equal sides. He took one more step forward, and his black eyes filled the broken mirror.

"And the sooner that I, the King of the Carnival, can get revenge for what was done to my queen."

ACKNOWLEDGMENTS

I'd like to thank Liza Fleissig, an amazing agent and a wonderful person. Endless gratitude to my editor, Christy Ottaviano, and her team for taking my sullied manuscript and polishing it until it shined. Xs and Os to my wife, who inspires me daily. This book is an homage to the great writers of chilling stories, including Ray Bradbury, Alvin Schwartz, Richard Matheson, and Stephen King. And finally, thanks to the kids who took the time and effort to read this book. I hope you found a few scares in here.

ANDREW NANCE

had a twenty-five-year career as a morning radio DJ. Today, he lives in historic St. Augustine, Florida, where he writes and is active in theater. He is the author of *Daemon Hall* and *Return to Daemon Hall: Evil Roots*.